Inside the Music

by

Jourdan Urbach

Library of Congress Card Number: 2004115815.

ISBN: 1-930648-98-7

First Printing, 2004

Published by
Goose River Press
3400 Friendship Road
Waldoboro ME 04572
dbenner@prexar.com
www.gooseriverpress.com

CONTENTS

Dedication

To My Teachers:

Ms. Patinka Kopec: For "raising" me to be a confident, bold and technically astute artist. What I have achieved, I owe to you.

Mr. Lewis Kaplan: For giving me permission to play the music my soul hears, and for unlocking the gypsy inside.

The days I've spent in your studios have been some of the finest moments of my life. I thank you both from the bottom of my heart. You've given me my voice.

CHAPTER 1

THE BEGINNING

Where does fame begin? It begins in a house just like this one.

I loved this house. It belonged to my grandma and zayde. I had a special place in it upstairs, tucked away in the corner under the eaves, with a bed and a bookcase, music stand, a desk, and casement windows to watch the world from inside. It was safe and contained. It was a place to be alone with myself, something I was never afraid of, and a place where I was close to two people I adored.

We had just arrived home from winter break and my parents allowed me to spend my last weekend before school started with my grandparents, even though my grandfather (zayde), was very sick. He was dying.

The rain began coming down in spotted streams of 16th notes, one-e-and-a, two-e-and-a, beat, beat, everything in life was sound and rhythm, pulses and lines, that's how I felt it. I could hear music in it all; in the creaking floor boards that carried the world in and out of my grandparents' home, in the lilt and crackle of a stranger's voice, in the words "I love you" from my parents' lips, in the washing machine when it changed cycles, in the layers and textures of my days. That's just how I was.

I pulled my bow across the strings. Thunder rolled off in the distance. It didn't scare me, but I had to stop playing for a moment. Normally, I wouldn't, but there was something particularly unsettling about that sound tonight, and the rain, too, for that matter. It's nothing I could express to you, it's just something I felt. A temporary shiver ran through me. I put down my violin and listened. The thunder howled like a spirit in the sky. Disturbing my solitude. Summoning change. My grandmother screamed.

I ran to the stairwell. "Grandma, what is it? What?"

"Zayde can't breathe. He's gasping, he can't catch . . . come down . . . hurry Joey . . . fast, fast."

I flew—tearing into the den where we had set up my zayde's hospital bed. My grandfather had pancreatic cancer, and he was told three weeks ago that he had three months to live. Three months—not three weeks! Why is he dying now? I want an appeal. It's too soon.

"Zayde, I'm here. Hold my hand. Look at me. Zayde, I'll play for you . . . wait I'll get my fiddle."

But he didn't turn to look at me. Why didn't he turn? He couldn't turn. He was leaving. Maybe he couldn't even hear me. He'd always make time to hear me play violin. The last few weeks, Grandma said my violin playing was keeping him alive. With each piece I'd watch his eyes fill with promises that he'd be there tomorrow when I'd come to play again; that he'd fight this infiltrator, this butcher, this disease that was stealing him from me. He'd rally, for those moments, and smile and twinkle. Such a zayde I had. There

2

never was such a man.

The rain continued. An occasional jab of lightening lit up the heavy, cloth curtains that kept him in my world. I looked down. He took a breath, his jaw dropped quickly as if someone's hand came and unhinged it. There was silence—no breathing—1, 2, 3, 4, 5. The jaw snapped back up again. This happened two more times. His jaw would pop down, as if it were a mechanical device, there would be an interminable number of seconds without the sound of breath, and then it would snap shut again.

"What's happening, Grandma?"

"He's shutting down, sweetheart. The life force is going out. He can't hear us now."

I watched him. I couldn't take my eyes off him. I waited...and hated myself for waiting. I came closer to the bed rails, clenching them, scared to move . . . scared that my movement might disturb the moments of life force still lingering in him. There was no more breath being drawn. I placed my hand on his arm. He felt so cold . . . so terribly cold. I moved his blanket higher up towards his neck. Why did I do that? What was I thinking? His eyes closed.

"I love you, Zayde."

My grandma wept and took his hand.

"Gershon, Gershon," she called.

I was alone. I felt the very heavy hand of God on my shoulder. He turned me to leave the room. To move on. Would I heed His call? I always used to think about what a trusting, pliable man the Biblical Abraham must have been. I mean, God called him and told him to take his only son and sacrifice him up on a mountain. First of all, did He think that by doing it on a mountain Abraham would feel closer to Him and would appreciate how small a thing a little son is? Did God think he could erase the child of Abraham's dreams with just a command. Who is God, after all? He didn't have to live Abraham's life and go through his sorrows, his quests, and his successes? Who is He to think that all successes and failures, fullness and emptiness reflect on Him and not on the person who is living the life? Who is this God who now pressed His heavy weight on my shoulder and slowly turned me away from my grandfather?

"I won't go, I tell you. You have no right! Where are you? Show yourself like a man and tell me why you took Zayde?" No answer.

He was my biggest fan. He was my good friend. I turned back around and reached for my grandmother. I held her—tight.

"I must notify people, Joey," my grandmother said, tears dropping in pear shaped diamonds from her beautiful eyes.

I didn't want to let her go. "In a minute, Grandma...please, in just a minute."

"Come ziskeit, let's go into the living room. I'll call for the people to come from the funeral home. They have to take Zayde soon, you know. You sit and wait for me."

I tried the couch; it just didn't do it for me. I couldn't stay still. I felt like I needed to be somewhere else. I walked over to the gently carved piano in the corner, covered with photos of Grandma and Zayde at all different times in their lives, and of my mom and dad and me. Pictures of me playing violin and Zayde pretending to conduct, pictures of Grandma and Zayde and me at my third birthday party with my first 16th sized violin, pictures of mom and dad at their wedding with a Grandma and Zayde I hardly recognized. The largest photo was one with my parents after my debut with the New Haven Symphony at Woolsey Hall. I ran my fingers across our faces. I was such a combination of those two. I looked like my dad, but had the musical soul and temperament of my mom. The Golub and the Cohen influences—there was no mistaking them.

My name is Josef Cohen, son of my mother (who is the daughter of my grandma, and sister of Uncle Mischa), the beautiful and very independent Rebecca Golub. My father is the fun-loving and very pragmatic David Cohen. My parents and I lived in the same town as my grandparents for thirteen years, Southbury, Connecticut.

I am thirteen years old, four feet, ten inches tall, slim build, with hazel eyes. I have wavy hair that is long and dark brown, almost black, but misses by a shade of intention. I have a fairly mellow personality except, I'm told, when I'm doing the things I'm most passionate about; then I tend toward the intensity of a jaguar right before the kill.

I began my violin studies at the age of three. That special "spark," they call it, was noticed by the time I was 6 years old. I began working two hours a day, and took two lessons a week with my teacher, Ms. Ida. She was wonderful. She didn't teach much technique but she brought out all the fire this little boy of six had to burn! She introduced me to Vivaldi and Bach, Hungarian Dances and La Folia. Music was such a joy with Ms. Ida.

My father, although not a musician, took my daily

practice routine very seriously. He would quiz my mother everyday to find out how I did, what I did, and for how long I did it. You see, my dad was a professor of mathematics at Yale University, but had always longed to make music. He says he just never had the talent.

My mother, on the other hand, came from a home where her brother was a prodigy (Uncle Mischa), and she had such negative feelings about the whole process of serious musical study and the damaging world of professional musicians, that she never even wanted to try. I could always tell, though, that she had great natural talent. She practiced with me every-day, and her comments were always dead on to what my teacher would want. She knew how to get the best out of me, even though she was probably cursing her-self for helping me to become what I was obviously put on this earth to do—something she believed, ultimate-ly, would hurt me.

"A double-edged sword," she used to say. "This tal-ent of yours is a great gift and a greater burden, Joey. You sure you want to be so involved in this?"

I never had any doubts. So, mom and I continued practicing till I won competition after competition, made a name for myself in Connecticut and then throughout the northeast. I played all the major halls in New England, from Jordan Hall in Boston to the beautiful and cavernous Woolsey Hall in Connecticut. They called me "prodigy," and we marked time until my teacher thought I was ready for New York.

By the time I was nine years old, I was considered ready. My parents allowed me to audition for the American Institute of Music, A.I.M. (one of the greatest conservatories in the world), and specifically for the great pedagogue, Lottie Liebling. I was accepted. My whirlwind musical career was about to take off.

My parents drove me every Saturday to A.I.M. It was a two hour drive. My first class was at 9:00 A.M. so we left at 7:00 A.M. This meant that I was up by 5:00 A.M., so that I could at least get one and a half hours of practice in before we left the house. It was such an ordeal. Grandma and Zayde told me that in a couple of years they would send me to live with Uncle Mischa in the city. Then I wouldn't have to commute on Saturdays and I could study with my teacher, Lottie Liebling, a few times a week, instead of on Saturdays and Wednesdays for two hours. My present schedule was not productive, grandma used to say.

Ms. Liebling had trained with the greatest, and she was known as the foremost authority on bow technique in the country. She had the reputation of being totally devoted to you, if you were accepted into her studio. By the time I reached thirteen, my present age, it was clear that we were devoted to each other. Grandma said that the stress I felt each Saturday would be greatly minimized if I lived in the city and could have more frequent lessons on weekdays, instead of having so much piled into a Saturday. Zayde said he would miss my Saturday visits, but that I'd just have to call and play for him on the phone. I shook my head dutifully. Everyone I knew respected Grandma's views on musical education because she had raised and nurtured Uncle Mischa to great heights in the field. I remember these conversations with them both like it was yesterday. It could have been.

My eyes passed from photo to photo. So many performances, so many special family occasions, such memories of happiness, and all with my grandfather present. I had to tell someone. Who was there to tell?

I ran upstairs to my room, sat down at the computer, and addressed an e mail to myself. Thank goodness for the computer—the great communication net. It can catch all your emotions as you're falling, put them in print, and never have anyone else know you were suffering. I pressed the e mail key. I typed only one sentence. . . . My Zayde died today. Pushed send. Anti-virus check. It was done. Zayde was sent out into cyberspace. I had expressed it. Shouldn't I feel closure? Shouldn't I feel something? Only numbness. Emptiness. I opened up my maroon binder and started my math homework.

It was Saturday night, January 13th. I had always stayed over my grandma and zayde's house on Saturday. It was the most relaxing, sweet part of the week. Even when Zayde became sick last month, I still came. I knew the time I had left with my grandfather was finite. But I couldn't think about that now. I had to remember all his stories, his sayings, his passion for music. How he loved it when I practiced for him every Sunday, and told him about my exploits at conservatory every Saturday evening. It would make him remember his son, my Uncle Mischa—once a great prodigy—and they saw me following the same path.

I had been spared the grueling five to seven hour a day practices with painful criticism by the top instructors in the world, because I didn't live the "music life" in Manhattan. My small town of Southbury was far from the realities of the American Institute of Music,

where I spent my Saturdays in the pre-college program. When I left the conservatory each Saturday
evening, I left that world behind—at least for the week.
Grandma and Zayde believed I could be even greater
than Uncle Mischa. . . . Mom feared that I would be.

There was a story I remembered word for word.
Grandma and Zayde practically raised me on the
story. My mom would remind me of the story any time
she could, in between school and my three hour daily
violin practice. It was a story with a lesson—one they
all wanted me to learn for their own personal reasons.
What that lesson was, you'll have to decide for yourselves.

CHAPTER 2

PLAYING FOR BERLINSKY

My Uncle Mischa had never gotten over a terrible misunderstanding that happened when he was thirteen years old. He was, by all family lore, one of the greatest, young concert violinists of his day. At thirteen, having spent five hours a day practicing, he had attained technical facility far exceeding others his age. For him the violin was life's very breath. He played with such passion, such musical ardor that anyone who heard him knew this was a talent to be reckoned with. So did his teacher, Dr. Pedagogia.

Pedagogia set up a recital opportunity for Uncle Mischa with, arguably, the greatest violinist of his day, Sascha Berlinsky. Uncle Mischa was absolutely on fire with anticipation. He didn't sleep for weeks, could barely eat. For the first time in his life all Mischa did was practice—hour after hour, taking breaks only for the sake of his weary, ever tightening muscles. Imagine how he felt knowing that one of his greatest dreams was about to come true. How many kids, thirteen years old, have this kind of opportunity? The great Berlinsky— known as much for his compassionate approach to young artists, as for his fiery fingers. All of life's great pleasures culminated in that one meeting. Uncle Mischa couldn't believe his luck.

So Mischa practiced grueling arpeggios and scales like he never had before, down-bows till his shoulder felt like jelly.

"More weight in the arm, Mischa. Your bow and fingers are never quite together. The bow!!! Make the bow do the talking! It's not all about the fingers. Speak to me with the bow," exclaimed his teacher. "Your rhythm! You can't do that to the rhythm. Who do you think you are? Heifetz? When you're Heifetz, then you can take liberties. Until then, do what the composer says." Pedagogia was merciless. It didn't matter how old Mischa was. He had to do it like an adult—now! "Ay! What will Berlinsky say? What will he do to you?" complained his teacher.

What would Berlinsky do to Uncle Mischa anyway? Hit him over the head with the bow? What was this man wailing about? Mischa was thirteen, not twenty. What he had, you couldn't buy in a violin store. So what if everything wasn't perfect? So what if he did things a little outside his teacher's method of technique to get his interpretation across? It was his. When you're thirteen, enjoying your music and doing your own thing is still very important. Surely even the greatest violinist was, at one time, a child. He'd understand.

"Ach, you will make mince meat of my name! What will Berlinsky think of me if I allow you to play that passage for him like this? You want to know what he'll think? I'll tell you what he'll think . . ."

Oh boy. Here it comes, thought Mischa.

"He'll think, what kind of teacher is this who would let a thirteen year old play the great repertoire like this?"

Ah, so there it was. It had nothing to do with him at all, thought Mischa. What an awful business this musical world is for one so young. You want to express the music in your heart, learn great repertoire, play for big audiences, and make your teacher happy as well.

Days of nerve wracking toil turned into weeks, and finally the day arrived. It was a Sunday afternoon—2:00 P.M.—just like a matinee. Mischa's mom, my grandma, had purchased a beautiful blue suit for the occasion, a crisp, white shirt, with just enough room under the arms (which a violinist always appreciates), and a deep cobalt blue, pinstriped tie.

My uncle spent twenty five minutes shining each shoe that day. Each one was a masterpiece. Grandma used to say that when Mischa shined his shoes on the day of meeting Berlinsky, you could see clear inside his heart, they were so clean.

So, Mischa drove with Grandma and Zayde two hours from Southbury to Manhattan, leaving at 8:00 in the morning. That means Mischa was up at 5:30 A.M. so he could warm up from 6:00 A.M. till 8:00 A.M. He had an 11:00 A.M. appointment with Berlinsky, but they didn't want to take a chance of being late.

"You never know with that tricky traffic," Grandma used to say.

All during the car ride, Mischa was busy rehearsing his fingerings. The fingers of his left hand flew up and down his right wrist as he tapped out the first movement of his concerto. It was the Brahms—the same concerto Berlinsky debuted at Lincoln Center sixty years earlier.

At 10:00 A.M. they pulled up in front of Berlinsky's building. The awning was deep green with white letters—The Beaufort.

"Oy, such a fancy name," remarked Grandma, "and so many floors. What do they need such floors for?"

"And you could be sure Berlinsky lives on the top," added Zayde. "Such a man belongs on the top."

I used to love hearing their remarks about this momentous visit.

An imposing doorman, garbed in hunter green (matching the awning), approached the car. There were gold epaulets all shiny and new, standing at attention on his shoulders. He stood regally by the front door of the car and opened it politely for Grandma.

"Oh, no, no no, sir, I'm not getting out. My son . . . he's playing for the great Berlinsky. Mr. Berlinsky, I mean," she repeated his name in hushed tones, as if she were talking about Reb Nachman of Bratslav.

"But, of course, madam," replied the doorman, without batting an eye. He wasn't impressed. He got to see Berlinsky everyday. He promptly opened the back door for Mischa.

"Ah, but, you see, we are just a little early, sir. Can we wait?" asked Grandma.

"Of course, mam. For how long?"

"Oh, just a little while—fifty, sixty minutes."

"I see . . . well mam, you'll have to move the car. You can't sit here for an hour."

"Okay, sir," Zayde chimed in, "No problem."

My grandfather proceeded to spend the next fifty-five minutes circling Berlinsky's block. No one said a word during that hour. At 10:55 A.M. they arrived again in front of the building. The doorman returned to the car and opened the back door ceremoniously.

"Now?" asked the doorman.

"Yes, now," Grandma piped up.

Mischa got out and never looked back. He was afraid if he saw Grandma's face, he'd remember his age and limitations and never regain his courage. The doorman shut the door of Zayde's car and led Mischa to the elevator. "Press P for the penthouse suite," enunciated the doorman with an explosive gust of air. You could feel the wind from that "p" all the way down the hall, thought Mischa. "Then turn left out of the elevator. You can't miss it."

So Mischa went through the shiny, mirrored elevator doors, pressed "p" and was off on a life changing adventure. As Grandma tells it, when Mischa arrived at the top floor and saw the massive mahogany doors of the penthouse on his left, he was momentarily paralyzed. Could he pull this off? Best not to think about it. Just press the bell. His right pointer pushed hesitantly on the buzzer. Suddenly he heard the entire first two lines of Eine Kleine Nacht Musik playing in the air.

"Oh my God, even his doorbell can play," thought Mischa. Startled but thoroughly energized, Mischa waited until the door opened.

"Ah, you must be young Mischa Golub. Come in, I've looked forward to hearing you."

My uncle began photographing every inch of the apartment that was in his plain sight. Snapping pictures with his mind, registering memories with his senses. On the left, in the entrance way, was a white wall lined with photos—the most precious photos. Each of a great violinist or conductor, and auto-graphed personally to Berlinsky. On the right was a long, low wooden bench laden with art objects from around the world. No doubt, thought Mischa, each had a story. Perhaps the President of Russia present-ed Berlinsky with one thing, perhaps the Queen of England gave him something else. Probably every con-cert he ever played had a token to remind him of it.

Directly in front of Mischa were two perfectly white French doors, leading them to a grand parlor. It must take great care to keep them so white, thought Mischa. As he entered, a nine foot grand piano—a Bösendorfer—lay before him. Its top was covered with pictures of . . . who else? Berlinsky. Berlinsky with pianists, Berlinsky with cellists, Berlinsky with the President. What a life, thought Mischa!

To the left were the fluffiest looking sofas he had ever seen, nine pillows on each—a row of huge ones, a row of medium size pillows, and a row of tiny fancy pillows. In front of them was an ornate Turkish look-ing mahogany coffee table, with delicately carved legs, and a grand, silky Turkish ottoman—beige and gold. To the right was a wall of bookcases, filled not with books, but with records—hundreds of records; ("prob-ably all of Berlinsky," Mischa thought).

"So what will you play for me young man?" Berlinsky asked, shocking Mischa out of his reverie.

"The Brahms, sir. I will play the Brahms Concerto."

Mischa was beginning to feel more confident. He pushed back his shoulders and felt as if he had grown a head taller. How nice this man seemed, this idol of his. Warm and open. Genuinely interested in the young man before him. Everything will be fine, thought Mischa.

He placed his case on the Turkish ottoman, not wanting to take a chance of scratching the mahogany table. He gave his bow a gentle swipe of rosin, curled his fingers for the down bow and went deep into that place all performers go when they play—inside the music. All you feel there is passion, all you hear is velvet, all you see is space. Time stands still. You are nothing—there is only the music. It was a spectacular place to be—away from the traffic, the noises of humanity, the ordinariness of furniture (although there was nothing ordinary about Berlinsky's furniture), away from the critique of teachers and critics, off in a world of perfect freedom, expression—the ultimate gift of God. He never wanted it to end. Was he doing all his fingerings correctly, was his bow straight, his vibrato even. Who knew? Who cared? He was there.

The last notes played themselves. The concerto was over. Mischa was afraid to look up. An explosion of applause rocked the parlor.

"Bravo, bravo young one! What emotion! What ideas! Where did they come from? So much talent. I'm very impressed. You must continue to work hard, you know. You will be very great. This is just the beginning for you—don't think this is it. You must do further work on your bow control, string crossings, legato, legato, legato. All these things will give your sound greater facility, more depth."

Mischa was shaking. Happy, but shaking.

"I loved that you tackled this concerto so early, and

that you were able to fill it with such meaning. No one can give that to you."

Mischa was awestruck. Berlinsky approved. He felt like shouting it from the highest mountain. BERLINSKY APPROVED.

"Thank you so much," Mischa bowed and said.

"What am I, a king that you bow to me? Never bow before another man, because there's always a possibility that you'll be greater. Will you remember?"

"Yes sir. I'll remember," laughed Mischa nervously.

"Keep up the wonderful work and promise you'll come back to play for me next year, yes?"

"Oh, yes sir, I promise," exclaimed Mischa, winded by his own exuberance.

He was back in the hallway. The mahogany doors closed behind him. He pressed the down button.

Grandma and Zayde were silent as he entered the car. They both turned their heads around to the backseat and stared at Mischa. Five or six seconds passed. Grandma couldn't take it anymore.

"So say something!!!"

Mischa smiled contentedly and looked at both of them for a split second that felt like hours.

"He approved. Berlinsky approved."

My grandparents beamed. What an honor had been bestowed upon their talented son. He would always be able to speak of this experience. If he never did another thing he would have this experience to remember. It was something he could be proud of his whole life.

When Uncle Mischa saw his teacher the next day he was quite pleased. Dr. Pedagogia had already spoken to Berlinsky.

"So, I hear my boy that you made quite an impression. He thought you were such a talent, and he wants to hear you in one year. Isn't that exciting?"

Of course Mischa knew all this already, but it made him happy to see his teacher so happy!

"You have that certain charisma in your playing, Mischa, just as I always told you. A certain flair. You are a performer. Berlinsky saw that! They don't all have that, my boy."

Dr. Pedagogia always called Uncle Mischa "my boy" when he was pleased with him. So all was well with the world. Pedagogia gave Mischa the O.K. to send out his resume and tape to all the major conductors in the country. It was time, he thought, for Mischa to play his Brahms with orchestra.

Mischa spent the next seven days typing up letters, duplicating his tapes and listing all his accomplishments of the past few years: competitions he had won (and there were several), solo recitals he had played, notices of critical acclaim he had received from performing in major halls, and one last thing that was foremost in his mind, that thing which marked the biggest day in his life—playing for Berlinsky.

Mischa sent out each letter with a headshot and a kiss for good luck. He knew it would take weeks, possibly months till he heard from any of these orchestras, but from everything he had been led to believe, he would definitely get called. He would wait.

Amazingly, Mischa began receiving calls within two weeks. Two, then three major orchestras got in touch immediately. They loved his tape and wanted to hear him in person. When could he come play for them? What were his bookings like for next year? They would make the appointments and speak to his teacher and a few others who had heard him and that would be the whole process. Mischa was overwhelmed and overjoyed. Grandma took the calendar in hand and made all the dates.

Then the strangest thing began to happen. Days before Mischa was scheduled to play in person for each conductor he received calls from their secretaries. They all said the same thing:

"We are terribly sorry, but we'll have to cancel due to circumstances beyond our control. Check with your teacher for details."

"Circumstances? What circumstances? All of them have the same 'beyond control' circumstances?" thought Mischa. "What has happened?"

"Why don't they want to hear my boy?" wept Grandma.

"Something out of Mischa's control has caused this," mused Zayde. "Some external source. They loved Mischa's playing. It doesn't make any sense."

Mischa's insides were burning. His head was swimming. His heart palpitated as if several iron workers were swinging their anvils inside his membranes. He cried. I don't know for how long, but Grandma said it was a sea of sadness in their home for the rest of that week. He couldn't eat, he drank sparingly. He couldn't look his parents in the face.

Saturday came, and Saturday was lesson day at Dr. Pedagogia's apartment. Mischa arrived on time, dutifully as ever. A storm was brewing. The clouds hung low in the sky like lids before a deep sleep . . . yearning to fall . . . presaging release. Mischa walked into the studio with a heavy heart. How could he tell his teacher that all his orchestral auditions had been cancelled? It turned out that he didn't have to.

"Mischa, how could you do such a thing?"

"What did I do now?" asked Mischa, weak and exasperated.

"You wrote down in your biographical letter to the conductors that you were invited to play for Berlinsky. Berlinsky doesn't like that. Why didn't you ask me about it before writing that? Why didn't you ask permission?"

Mischa's head was spinning. Ask permission for what? For telling the truth about such an important life event? It may not have meant anything to Berlinsky, but it meant everything to him!

"So the conductors won't see me because they know Berlinsky doesn't like his name linked to any students he doesn't teach?" Mischa hypothesized.

"No, the conductors won't see you because Berlinsky won't let them. They called to ask him what he thought of you, since you used his name on your resume. Berlinsky was fuming. If there's one thing he can't stand, it's when students use him as a stepping stone, trying to impress people by linking his name with theirs."

"What kind of a stepping stone? What are you saying? I'm thirteen. I was excited. It was a big moment in my musical life! I didn't say he thought I was the next Heifetz, or that he thought anything in particular about me . . . just having been approved to play for him was big enough for me. That belongs in my bio. Not everyone gets to have that experience. It should make him feel good that it meant so much to a thirteen year old boy. Wouldn't it make you happy to know you had such an affect on a young student that they wanted to include playing for you in their bio?"

"He doesn't look at things that way. You just should have asked me to read your bio—before you sent it out."

"So there is nothing in my life I can do without prior approval? Nothing I can do in my musical career without asking someone's permission first? Soon I'll be afraid to call myself a violinist without asking permission, because maybe I should have said a 'violin student.' " Mischa had never spoken out like this before. His teacher was dumbstruck. "What did he do to me? What did he say to them?" Mischa prodded.

"He said that they are not allowed to engage you because you used his name, and he doesn't want to be linked to every student he hears in his career—he feels he is being used. Oh Mischa, it hurts me so to tell you this. I never thought such a thing would happen to you when I arranged that meeting. Never."

"What can I do to fix it, Dr. Pedagogia? Just tell me and I'll do it."

"Nothing, I'm afraid. It's over."

My uncle had nothing else to say. He was ruined. He tried to keep his spirits up over the next few weeks, telling himself that perhaps other orchestras he had sent tapes to would soon call. But they never did. Mischa sunk deeper and deeper into depression. Grandma could no longer pick up the pieces. Mischa stopped going to see Dr. Pedagogia, and stopped playing violin. He finished high school and went on to college just like any other kid. Inside he carried with him, though, the secret that he was not like any other kid.

He could have been extraordinary. It's funny how greatness can make one life and destroy another.

Years passed and Mischa wound up teaching violin. He had studied philosophy in college but I guess he never found the answers he was looking for. He was, heart and soul, a musician, no matter what he studied or attempted. He, ironically, became a sought after teacher because he had maintained his wonderful technique and beautiful musical ideas. It was a rare combination in a teacher. He taught with great kindness, Grandma always said, but never offered to make an introduction for any of his students to play for the new, great artist of the day—the flavor of the month. He knew better.

"If you want to send your tapes out, go ahead, and my best wishes are with you. If a conductor wants to call and talk to me about your repertoire—that's fine, too, but you're on your own. I'd rather you play for the love of the art, than the need to be famous. That way, you'll never get hurt. The music itself will never hurt you."

Stories emerged over the last few years as if they were creeping out from behind dusty, dirty, Venetian blinds. Stories about Uncle Mischa and his forays into the world of Kabbalah and magic. Word had it that Uncle Mischa would disappear for days at a time without notifying his students. They'd ring and ring until they had to get the land lady to open the door. Mischa wasn't there. He'd return some days later and continue with his lessons as if he'd never been gone. No one knew where he had been. He'd never say. If someone asked, he'd pretend he hadn't heard them and continue beating time with his baton on the music stand.

So this was the environment I grew up learning about, and the one that, ultimately nurtured me and taught me the ropes. My grandma had always told me that in time, when I was ready, she would send me to live with Uncle Mischa in Manhattan so that I could study and attend the American Institute of Music more regularly. It was my destiny, she said, like it was his—except I would have the good fortune of having learned from Uncle Mischa's mistakes.

CHAPTER 3

THE CARNIVAL OF THE KIDS

As it stood, on weekdays, I woke up at 5:30 A.M., began practice with Mom by 6:00 A.M., and worked till 8:00 A.M. at which time I grabbed my school books and left for public school. I spent three and a half hours a day at school, where truly no one understood what I was about, and then returned home either to complete my practice, have an accompanist rehearsal with Luba (my accompanist), or travel into the city for a second lesson with Ms. Liebling. It took a real bite out of my social life, but that's what serious, young professional musicians did.

Have you ever heard a sweeter more musical name: Lottie Liebling? It was a grand one, for a grand lady. Usually I'd see her on Wednesdays and Saturdays—splitting the hours of difficult coaching. My repertoire was so large, it required a couple of days a week just to hear everything.

I remember when all I had were two pieces in my repertoire that I could play, I thought, flawlessly. That was when I had first auditioned for Ms. Liebling. She had me stand in the middle of her studio and said, "Now schatsy," (that was German for little creature—a special term of endearment she used), "you play your first piece and I'll be listening and watching your technique as you play. Just remember to always face me while you're playing, okay?"

I nodded my head and began to play. As I played, Ms. Liebling began moving around me in circles—so I followed her. She turned left, I turned left. She turned right, I turned right. She stopped, I stopped. This went on for nearly half a page of my piece. Suddenly, she burst out laughing. "Schatsy, what are you doing? Why are you following me?"

"You said to always face you when I played, so that's what I was doing," I answered, unsure why I had caused such gleeful hysteria in my teacher. I didn't know that I had turned a full 360 degrees from the time I began the piece. "See, I couldn't face you when you were behind me, so I kept moving," I added. It seemed perfectly logical to me.

By this time Ms. Liebling was doubled-over. "No, no Joey, I didn't mean you had to play and follow me around the room. I just wanted you to start off facing me and stay that way. I was looking for specific technical problems in your bow arm."

"Did you find them?" I asked courteously

"Who could find them? I was too busy watching you following me in circles." She laughed so heartily. Ms. Liebling enjoyed herself tremendously that day. I was happy to oblige.

It took me a few months to understand all the details Ms. Liebling wanted from me. We made each other laugh so many times before we thoroughly got to know each other. It was the perfect student-teacher relationship. She never knew what would come next with me, and I never knew how she'd take it. I could spend a ½ hour trying to get Ms. Liebling to accept my interpretation or bowing for a segment of a piece. I'd look forward to my ride to A.I.M. twice a week, so I'd have extra time to gather my didactic ammunition. We were both stubborn creatures, so I knew early on, finding a compromise would not necessarily make either of us happy musically. One had to sell the other on his/her idea, and eventually one party would accept. Sometimes Ms. Liebling's ideas won and sometimes mine actually won. It was exhausting, but part of the "Democratic" musical process.

I had a similar novice type experience with my other teacher, Professor Krantz in my early days at A.I.M. His specialty was working on the musical interpretations of pieces with me. I remember, I was working on Zigeunerweisen with him. The goal was to make it sound as gypsy-like as possible. It's a fabulous piece written by Sarasate, in the "gypsy mode." The first part is improvisational, dark and romantic; the last part is "break-neck speed" fast, and exciting.

Professor Krantz definitely had the right personality to work on this piece. When we got to the last section he said, "Now try to imitate me. This is the spirit you're going for." He picked up the fiddle and began firing off the notes at 100 m.p.h.—all while he danced and swayed, his head nodding, his eyes shining, his feet tapping. He was, for that moment, a gypsy. "Hai diddle hai, hai, deedidee-dee...Hey!" He sang between the florid passages.

How did he do that? Sing and play and do a little jig, all at the same time? I figured that's what he wanted from me, so. . . . "Here goes nothin'. . . . Hey, hai, ha." My feet started moving, my head was nodding gently and before I knew it, I was doing a little dance across the living room floor. Now, I don't want you to think I was often given to spontaneous outbursts of Hora. I just got a little carried away! I caught Professor Krantz's face out of the corner of my eye. His smile was as wide as a city block.

"Ho, ho . . . look at you. You're a gypsy."

These were the splendid memories of making music in the studios of my teachers that I'd have for the rest of my life.

It really would be the perfect plan to live there in the city. Although I can't imagine being without my mom and dad for a semester—let alone my grandmother. I felt them all supporting this move, pushing me toward some greatness. *Would it ever be achieved,* I wondered?

So hard not to disappoint people who have given you everything. The guilt burns so brightly you could light a potbelly stove in winter with it. This is the universal guilt that exists among prodigious violin students. It's kept under wraps in fine tuxedos and long black concert skirts, but it exists. It comes out when the gowns and suits have been hung up in the closets and you are left bare—you and your guilt. You may reach for it and caress it and make it work for you up on that stage, or you can examine it too carefully and get the "kishkes" kicked right out of you on the same stage. Ultimately, you realize this is for you, not for them, even though you love them to death. In the end it has to be about you.

We all have different ways of dealing with the guilt, the pressure, the grandness of the adventure. You wouldn't expect some of the things I'm about to tell you regarding our lives, but you're going to hear them anyway because you picked up this book. I owe it to you.

The stories—everybody had one. There was Lavinia, whose mother was Chinese and whose father was Spanish. We were never quite sure if each really understood what the other was saying, but it didn't seem to matter. They were bound together by the same celestial goal—world domination of the solo violin industry.

Once you learned to interpret their game, you could actually be a playful participant. The game went like this: When there was a performance, the mother made sure everyone knew that Lavinia had very little time to practice. "Only an hour yesterday, poor thing," her mother would say. This was an attempt to make those of us who did our requisite three hours a day of practice, feel smaller than a sound post.

Or you might hear that something almost devastating happened to her violin the day before, like the bridge moved or two strings popped at once (which never happens!). These "near death" incidences concocted by the mother served to make Lavinia's performance that day even more wonderful in the eyes of those who heard the tales of woe. So, all you needed to do to play the game was shake your head from side to side and say things like "wow," "no kidding," or "oh my, what will she do now?"

Yes, Lavinia's mother was a veteran actress. She'd frown and wring her hands outside the recital hall at A.I.M., exclaiming that she was just too nervous to sit in the hall to hear her daughter perform. In reality, she was making sure no one would enter the hall late, and thereby possibly make a noise to distract Lavinia from her command performance.

Lavinia was no angel in this endeavor either. At our last orchestra auditions, dozens of us tried out for concert and assistant concert master/mistress (which are the two most honored seats in the orchestra). My best friend, Catherine and I got the positions. Lavinia spent the whole day complaining that the only reason she didn't get the seat was because she had sprained her leg three weeks earlier and it still hurt when she stood on it to play. You know what my reaction was? Go tell that to Itzhak Perlman!

The next component of the game was how Lavinia dressed. Even though she was twelve, she dressed as if she were six—with little pig tails, red bows, long frilly dresses, and little white dress socks with lacy little scalloped edges. Too cute! Yes, even patent leather shoes. There's actually a whole school of thought about dressing "under age" in our business. Appear as young as possible for as long as possible, then you not only astound the audience with your prodigiousness, but you have the "ooooh—ahhhh—how adorable" factor working for you as well. It's a living!

I often found myself feeling sorry for Lavinia. What must life have been like for her? I'd quickly catch myself, however. After all, this was part of a carefully calculated plan—prodigiousness is always calculated.

Thank God for Mr. Herrington—Francis Scott Herrington. He was the conductor of our orchestra. He was 5'2" tall and a rather compact human being. Balding, except for his salt and pepper pony tail, which swept down his back, as regal as a lion's mane. He would say, "If you practice one hour a day, you're a fool. If you practice more than three, you're a bigger fool!" If you were lagging behind in your rhythm he'd insist that you had eaten too much cafeteria food. And if the kids were particularly noisy, he'd whack his baton on the stand and say in a whisper, "I want everyone to be really quiet so you can hear the cockroaches plotting to destroy Juilliard." (Every conservatory was fair game for Herrington, except his own.)

Something you couldn't miss about Mr. Herrington was the way he dressed—the socks always matched the shirt. You should'a seen him on St. Patrick's Day. Actually, the scariest day was Valentine's Day . . . red shirt, a bow tie with red and white hearts, and red socks with little white hearts on them—one shudders to think what else might be matching!

Mr. Herrington's favorite line came when someone wasn't watching his conducting closely enough. "I don't understand why you wouldn't want to look at me. I'm the handsomest guy in the room." That would start him on a comic tirade, and you could count on at least five minutes of musical one liners . . .

"I have to stare at all you little bohemian wannabes all the time, but you get to stare at me, the most beautiful person in the orchestra! Hey, Oblows! Stop buying your reeds at Wal-Mart. If you keep this up I'll have to send you to Curtis." (Curtis Institute is, along with Juilliard and the American Institute of Music, one of the greatest conservatories in the world.) "Do you know what the difference is between a cello and a coffin? A coffin has the corpse on the inside, and a cello has the corpse on the outside." (He had something against cellists. I still can't figure it out.) "Yung-Li, you're looking very old-ly today!"

One of the funniest days was the first day of

orchestra in September. Mr. Herrington was calling
the role and learning to match faces with names. He
started with the first violins, "Chan, Chang, Chin,
Chung, Cohen . . . COHEN? . . . Who let you in?"

Well, you get the idea. I, personally, will miss him
terribly when I move up to the next orchestra. He had
a big bark, but was really a pussy cat; I can't imagine
a more colorful maestro anywhere. Oh, and by the
way, he was a superb conductor. It's just that his personality was larger than the entire field of classical
music.

We all lived in fear of the next year—moving up to
Maestro Vunderfall's orchestra. You couldn't make a
crack there. Not a sound could be heard except his
baton tapping and metal chairs being tossed off the
stage into the first two rows—and that was on a good
day. You didn't want to get on his bad side, or you'd
still be sitting on the chair when he tossed it. That's
how he'd get your attention. Nice, huh?

"You vill vatch da markings in da music or you vill
end up on da street corner vith a monkey!" It was a
favorite of his. Ah, American Institute had a million of
'em!

Then there was Valery Maeskofsky, the elder. Of
course the elder implies that there was a younger, but
there wasn't. He was just one of the older boys in the
program—seventeen to be exact. I called him Mr.
Machismo. He was just such a "type"—one out of an
old Russian novel or something, who needed a special
appellation or appendage to his name. Piercing deep
brown eyes, long, sleek, black hair that crested at his
shoulders, cut upper body, from practicing 5 hours a
day. Valery was the boy all other boys wanted to be,

and all girls wanted to be with. "Music is my life," he'd say with his thick Russian accent, swinging his scarf over his left shoulder and exiting the room. The guy sure had presence. When he came onto the stage, the whole first 5 rows were pre-packed with "feline" admirers, swooning in "cut time."

Valery really knew how to play a crowd, too. Of course some violinists play the audience better than they do their violins, but that was not the case with Valery. He was gifted in both arenas. First, he'd strike a pose when he came out on stage. Then he'd walk over to the piano and take just a little longer than necessary tuning his strings, always with his best side facing the audience. He'd hold his violin scroll up in the air at the ends of movements just a little higher than the rest of us—for maximum drama. When he'd take his bows, he stayed down just a little longer than the rest of us—to ensure optimum applause time.

Among my cohorts in music was Noah Steiger. Noah was a nice enough kid. He was thirteen, with blonde curly hair springing from his scalp like small slinkys and very Aryan looking eyes. Now the thing about Noah was his self-esteem problem. Noah was an excellent violinist—superb technically. He worked hard, but he didn't have the innate artistry of others.

Noah felt that very deeply. So every time there was a performance class, in which Ms. Liebling's students had to each get up and perform their latest piece with accompanist, Noah would beg to be last, and be cowering and whimpering through the whole hour. That is, until his turn, at which point we'd all be awaiting his, by now, trite mantra."They all sound better than me. I didn't get enough time to practice with the accompanist. I won't sound good."

Often, the tears would just begin running down his cheek, as if they had a mind of their own. Noah had been pulling this for so long, he couldn't help himself. Even if he wanted to take a deep breath and go up there like a pro, he couldn't. He had too much invested in this persona of his—this "poor little me" thing.

The teachers would all feel sorry for him because he lacked self-esteem. The students would all give him hugs and treat him like their brother or something. Noah couldn't change if he tried. Unfortunately, I couldn't help feeling that Noah was really manipulating us all. He was a very bright boy, too bright not to see how his actions affected people. If he couldn't be the best, or second best, he'd be the persecuted one. Everyone's got a shtick!

Amidst all this insanity was Catherine—a tall slender girl with blue-gray eyes, long brown hair, and a neck made to hold a Stradivarius. When her wrist pulled the bow, it was like watching poetry, and her sound flowed with an organized sweetness that took years to cultivate. She was a calm, quiet soul—went through life with grace, something every musician longs for. If she felt the heat of competition, I certainly never knew it. Somehow she managed to have friends, maintain an A average in school, and be one of the top violinists at the institute. She and I were always up for the same awards and competition prizes, but I never minded. I admired her.

Another wonderful character in our conservatory life was Dr. Lydian, the theory teacher. Dr. Lydian was from Princeton initially, but yearned to be where the music never stops. Well, he sure got that by coming to us. He blustered about the classroom, leaving torrents of theory behind. By the end of class there wasn't a spot on the board that hadn't been written on. The truly annoying thing is that he only used the marker board, and every ten minutes or so his markers would run dry, so he'd spend the next five minutes fishing through his bag for fresh ones. An admirable use of class time.

He periodically turned to make sure we were all still there; those who were awake, smiled dutifully and nodded . . . nodding is good. It's one of those survival tactics in class that keeps the teacher happy and engaged.

One day, Catherine and I met for a moment in the hall. "Did you hear what happened to Salvador in Herrington's orchestra?"

Salvador started classes at 8:00 A.M. every Saturday with his private instrumental lesson (poor guy), and he didn't even have five minutes for a bathroom break until 1:30 P.M. when orchestra was over. So he'd usually race to orchestra, have his stand partner time him each week as he darted to the bathroom and back in time for Mr. Herrington's downbeat. Each Saturday he tried to beat his best time from the weeks before. This week, I guess it didn't work.

"He didn't make it there on time to get to the bathroom and back, so he just held it."

"What do you mean he held it? For two hours?"

"Yep. What a guy!" We laughed.

"I saw him chugging down the hall with pained grimaces on his way to the men's room."

"OOOOO—Out of the way! No time to Lose!" I added gleefully.

Catherine giggled all the way to ear training class. I loved making her laugh. I kept a mental notebook of all the great anecdotes I heard in the halls and class-rooms, just so I could relay them to her in between classes.

Evidently, Salvador had a banner day. He was fool-ing around in theory before class started, crawling through the attached "desk/chair" components, and somehow got himself stuck. Much to Dr. Lydian's dis-may, upon entering class he was greeted by Salvador's ample bottom sticking up out of the chair. I would've sat through another period of theory just to see that!

After dropping Cat off at ear-training class, I con-tinued down the halls towards the elevators and bumped into Lavinia. "Hey Joey. Did ya' hear? The first semester jury grades are in. I know your grade if you're interested. I got all A+s."

"Wait a minute. You know your grade and you know my grade, but I don't know my grade. What's wrong with this picture?"

Lavinia just looked down at her feet and smiled coquettishly.

"Do you know what other people got too, or am I just special?" I asked, looking her right in the eye.

You see, ever since Lavinia got to school, she's been trying to pull ahead of me in something—any-thing! Imagine putting all that stress on one young boy? I'm positively exhausted! Anyway, our charming and alarming conversation continued.

"Look, I'll tell you what you got if you want. In fact, you should know that I really got an A++ 'cause there seems to be an extra plus next to one of my A+s on one of the judge's sheets. That must mean something, right? That must mean I got higher than 100, don't ya think?"

"Well, maybe it was a stray mark," I added nauseously.

"But no, there were definitely two crosses there next to the A," she assured me.

"So maybe there were two stray marks!" I was really losing my patience now.

"Well," she tossed her hair nonchalantly, "I'll have to ask Ms. Liebling about it. I'll let you know, okay?"

"Oh, be sure to do that," I added.

I wanted to get onto a moving elevator going anywhere away from Lavinia just about then, but I couldn't stand the suspense. I had to know. After all, it was my grade and she had it. How could I wait two more classes to find out from my teacher? I know what you're thinking. How could I, Joey Cohen, man of the people, play into her hands like that? Well, I just did. Don't want to discuss it anymore.

"So Lavinia, how did I do?"

"Oh, you got an A+, too. You wanna' know your comments?"

"You know my comments?"

"Sure, whose do you want first?"

"You memorized them by professor?" How did she get the time? She really needs to get out more.

"I just have a great short-term memory. I'm gifted that way," she added.

By this time, her pigtails were beginning to look very much like levers . . . and I felt the need to PULL!

"Okay. What did Maestro Vunderfall say?" I started with the toughest first, since I knew they wouldn't get any worse than his.

"Actually he said you have the makings of a great solo artist, that you're a fiery and exciting player. I didn't get that in my comments. I wonder why."

"I'm sure it was an oversight," I said, beginning to feel quite magnanimous.

"He did mention that at the end in the cadenza you took too many liberties with rhythm for his taste."

"But it's a cadenza. You're supposed to take liberties." I countered.

"Yes, well, you know he's a metric man, loves his rhythm. So anyway, he obviously still thought there was room for improvement."

"Okay. You've been very helpful. I'll find out the rest from Ms. Liebling," I said.

The elevator arrived right on time. We parted ways on the 4th floor. As I got off, I ran into her mother. "Joey, congratulations. I heard you did outstanding on your juries. They said you'll be a great soloist." She paused. I was waiting for the inevitable follow-up. "Of course, you know Lavinia popped two strings the night before the juries. She had to put on two new ones, and you know how strings go out of tune for days when they're new. Ah, we were so upset. I can't believe she even made it through."

"Wow! No kidding! But she got an A+, too," I said.

"Actually an A++," added her mother sheepishly.

"Yeah, that's what I heard."

"Of course she has to check that with Ms. Liebling. We're not exactly sure what it says."

"Oh, I'll be happy to check it for her, if you like."

"No, no, no, it's all right," said her mother. "I'll check later."

"Of course," I said knowingly. "See ya."

I tore down the hall straight to my teacher's studio. So I'd be 5 minutes late for ear training. I had to see my jury sheets. I knocked twice and Ms. Liebling invited me in.

"Ah schatsy I'm so proud of you. You got all A+s."

"I know," I responded cheerfully.

"How did you know, schatsy?"

"Lavinia told me."

"But how did she know?" Ms. Liebling asked quizzically. "Oh, that's what was taking her so long to find her sheets. She was reading yours—checking out the competition." Ms. Liebling laughed. She always encouraged a little healthy competition among her students. She said it made them play better. "Did you hear what Maestro Vunderfall said about you?"

"Of course I did."

"Of course you did." We both laughed uncontrollably.

So first semester had come to a successful close. I did my best, and it paid off. I gave Ms. Liebling a hug and ran off to ear training class. I couldn't wait to tell Catherine later.

After class, I tried the 5th floor, then the fourth floor, no luck. I bolted down to the second floor, where there were practice rooms, but the only one I found was Lavinia. I heard her playing the first line of the first movement of her concerto over and over. I peaked through the small glass window in the practice room, and sure enough, there she was with her mother. As I reached for the knob, a blast of Mandarin spiraled its way toward the glass pane. I couldn't understand what was being said, but I knew it wasn't good. Suddenly, recognition...

"OUT OF TUNE!"
Lavinia repeated the line with bold strokes.
"OUT OF TUNE! OUT OF TUNE!"
Lavinia retook her bow and began again.
"I say, out of tune, you lazy girl."
More gusts of disappointment sprayed into the air and collapsed at Lavinia's feet. She composed herself and began again. Her eyes hung low, her cheeks were flushed and the tears, imminent. I felt for Lavinia. A flash of my last practice with my mom blinded me momentarily. I saw her arms flailing before me, conducting each passage of my concerto.

"No, no, slow the tempo, for the twentieth time, slow the tempo. The orchestra has to slow down here, and you have to be the one to do it. You think the conductor is going to retard without his soloist? You must take control. You don't take control of your tempi, you lose the orchestra; you lose the orchestra, you make a fool of yourself in front of your audience; you make a fool of yourself, you get bad reviews; with bad reviews, comes death to the artist!"

Why did I have to replay that? There were so many wonderful things about practice with my mom, why do I have to keep hearing that over and over in my head? Death to the artist! Just what a thirteen year old needs to hear. What is it with these adults?

More Mandarin . . . then, "What's wrong with you? You were supposed to practice this with open strings yesterday. You lied to me. How you supposed to play perfect without perfect intonation? How you be big star with intonation problem? You never learn, girl. You no achieve nothing."

Lavinia burst into tears, speaking in hushed tones

as a sea tumbled over her cheeks. Death to the artist. I left quietly, but with a heavy heart.

I eventually found Catherine at the end of the never-ending hall of practice rooms on the second floor. We exchanged jury successes. I wanted to tell her what I had observed in Lavinia's practice room, but I just couldn't. I needed to talk about it, so why couldn't I do it with my best friend? What was the point of having one? The words wouldn't come. Bottle 'em up. It's growing pains, right? Sure.

I had wanted to ask Catherine to lunch all semester. Actually, I had wanted to ask her any where all semester but let's face it, it's hard for a guy. She was my ally, my buddy—who wants to screw that up? But what am I supposed to do—deny my feelings? I was a healthy, red-blooded, American male—a musician, no less . . . lots of feelings! It was end of semester. I should give it a shot, right?

"So Cat, you wanna go somewhere for lunch today? You know, celebrate end of juries?"

"Cool, great idea. I even have money today. Where should we go?"

"Don't worry, I have enough for both of us. How about the Noodle Shop?"

"Awesome. I never get to eat there. All the college kids go."

"Great! I'll meet ya in the lobby in a half hour. I just have to practice the last page of my third movement."

"See ya at the guard's desk in thirty minutes." Catherine disappeared back into her practice room.

Oh yeah, oh yeah! I did my little victory dance down the corridors. It was turning into a good day after all.

Cat and I met in the lobby after practice, started toward the door, and then...

"Yoohoo! Guys! Wait up!"

Oh no, it was Lavinia. No, no, no, no—not now. I absolutely was not up to being charming now. I needed all my "charming" for Catherine.

"Oh, hey, Lavinia," I kept moving slowly backwards towards the door.

"You guys going to lunch?"

"Uh, yeah." Her eyes were still slightly swollen from doing battle with her mom.

"Swell, I'm starving. Where are we going?"

Swell? First of all, who says "swell" anymore? Second of all, what was up with this "we" business. "We" were not going anywhere. I, however, was going somewhere with Catherine.

"We're headed to the Noodle Shop, but we don't have much time till end of period."

I felt ashamed as I looked into her beleaguered face. I was scum.

"Oh . . . it's really okay for me, though. I've got the same fifty minutes as you guys. We'll all rush back together. I've got to get out of this place."

"I know what you mean," I offered.

We left . . . together . . . foiled!

We got a prime table by the kitchen at the Noodle Shop. The aroma of steaming miso soup wafted across the room. Lavinia let it all out.

"That woman hates me. I swear she hates me."

"Who?"

"My mother. She went ballistic on me today—in the practice room—where everyone could hear outside

41

in the corridor. I'm never forgiving her. That's decided right now."

"What happened?" I feigned ignorance because I didn't want Lavinia to know I had heard the whole thing.

"She insists I didn't work on my intonation yesterday. She heard me in my room for 2 hours. She heard me checking with open strings. I did my best. It's not like I want to be out of tune. So, the first note that sounded a little off today, she lost it on me. I'm telling you, the woman hates me."

"How come she wasn't working with you yesterday? Doesn't she always?" Catherine asked.

"Yeah, but she was letting me try one practice a week by myself. A little autonomy—finally. That's finished now, you can be sure. She'll never trust me anymore. It has to be perfect, always perfect."

Lavinia was so agitated, her face had become crimson and swollen.

"You know what the last straw was for my mother? When my friend, Su-jin, from Juilliard, got accepted for representation."

"You mean, like, she has an agent?" Catherine queried in disbelief.

"Yeah, some big shot from ICM. Can you imagine? She'll be traveling all over the world by next year. My mother was ready to kill someone. She's been haranguing me for the past week every day: 'how come she got agent? She in better place, Juilliard? They more aggressive there for students? I didn't think so. AIM, great conservatory. Why not agent find you here? You have same talent!' "

"Whoa, how did you handle that?" I asked, feeling

very sorry for Lavinia by now.

"I just left the room. I would have left the house if I could drive . . . ooh, I can't get away from this woman!"

"Do you want representation now, Lavinia?" Catherine asked. "That's kind of the end of your 'student' life, you know? Maybe also the end of stressless learning. You'll be wolfing down lots of repertoire for performance all the time. That's not always so great for a student."

"I don't know. It would be kinda' cool to tour—just a little. I wouldn't have to do it all the time," Lavinia said pensively.

"That's just not reality, Lavinia. Once an agent gets his hands on you, you are pretty much beholden to all the gigs he accepts for you. It's a lot of pressure," I added. "Do you really want that at twelve years old?"

"Look, my life is plenty stressful. You guys just have no idea. Sometimes I'm sorry I got started with this whole thing. At least I'd know whether my family loves me for myself or for what celebrity I can bring them. Although, with my mother, if I didn't show talent on an instrument, she'd probably have me in an ice skating rink four hours a day!"

Cat and I just looked at each other. I didn't know what to say. Not that I haven't had issues with my mother and her drive for perfection. It's just that we had a totally different relationship. Healthy—I think you'd call it. But Lavinia's situation—it was a whole other "animal." I felt myself breaking out into a sweat. Maybe the heat from the kitchen.

Catherine regaled Lavinia with annoying stories of her little brother—how he'd stand outside her practice room singing, "La,la,la" at different pitches for minutes at a time, just to try to throw her off. Her mother would always side with the brother because she didn't want Joshy to feel he wasn't special too. So, it seemed, no matter what he did, he never got taken to task for it. Catherine was pretty fed up with that. I watched her speaking, but after a while I only saw her lips moving. The words just didn't seem as important. Some lunch this turned into. Noodles and aggravation. It was time to leave.

CHAPTER 4

DEPARTURES & ARRIVALS

Well, this was my life and these were the people who lived it with me. It was a colorful, hectic, sometimes stressful existence, but always an adventure, and never boring. I was thankful for that part, especially during the week of Shiva—those first seven days following the death of a loved one, when friends and relatives come to your house to express their sorrow and review memories with you about your dearly departed. When my grandmother wasn't deep in conversation with estranged family members or good friends, she sat with the catalogue from A.I.M. (American Institute of Music). She'd point out all the wonderful courses I could take at the conservatory if I had more time during the week.

"Oh Becca, he'll thrive in the city. He can see Ms. Liebling whenever he needs. She has taken such good care of him so far, I trust her to steer Joey's career."

"I hope you're right Mom. We're all giving up a great deal here. I'm giving my son into someone else's hands for a semester—that's a semester of his growth, emotional development, and social adventures I won't be a part of. Talking your heart out on the phone is not a substitute for being there and holding his hand."

Mom was not in any way convinced that this was

the time for me to go full gear into music study, but she stood aside for me. She knew it was what I dreamed of, and Mom was never one to stand in the way of a dream.

My mother had been a professional writer before I was born. She wrote hundreds of articles for magazines and journals—fiction, non-fiction, what ever they handed her, she could do. She even won prizes in the field—but always for her shorter works. Mom had dreamed, since college, of writing that one novel—the great "Connecticut novel," she would laugh and call it. She had so many wonderful first chapters from her days at Yale. She just somehow never took the time to nurture them into full scale novels. Eventually, she chose instead, to nurture me into a full scale musician.

Who knows the reasons we do things in life? Who knows what she was looking for? If you ask her, she might even tell you she's found it. All I know is, Mom has allowed me to be an artist in every kernel of my being, in what I put into my music, in what I bring away from studies, in how I view the communicated word and sentiment. She brought me up to find my place . . . and now it was time to go there.

I couldn't even tell you where the days began and ended that week. They seemed to move so quickly now. I kept a calendar by my bedside to mark the units of time before I was to begin my adventure.

My mom helped me pack the night before the great journey.

"You want these two sweatshirts, hon? It's going to be pretty cold for the next few months."

"I know, yeah, I'll take them both. Do you think I

should pack summer things for May?"

"I wouldn't. It really doesn't get that warm until the beginning of June, and you'll be home by then. You could take two pairs of shorts with your T-shirts, if you want. But it's so much clothing. Better to keep it light."

"Okay. I'll just take a pair of shorts, then."

"You've got to get a porter to help you with the bags at the station, okay? Promise me. You could hurt your shoulder, Joey. Don't try to be macho with all this stuff to carry."

Mom was deep into the folded laundry. She didn't look at me once.

"Mom, are you going to miss me?"

Pause . . . no words came.

"Mom?"

"What do you think? This was not my idea, you know. I can't stand that you're going; you're too young for all this. You have no idea the kind of pressure you'll be under, living with Mischa and practicing with him. He's certifiable, you know. I mean, he's a good person and all, and very loving, otherwise I'd never send you, but he'll work you like you're the disciple of Paganini! It will be stressful for you Joey. Expectations will be rising faster than the rate of inflation."

My mother was crying now.

"Will I miss you? I'll miss you terribly."

I hugged my mother till all my questions were answered. It would be hard to be away . . . it would be harder not to.

"If you have any doubts, Joey, there's no shame in waiting a year or two. Your gift and your career will be there at 14 or 15, you know."

"I have no doubts, Mom. I have to do this now. It's what I've been preparing for, right?"

Mom looked at me as if my future was too much for her to bear. It was a look of great love and devotion . . . and knowing. "Okay. It's what you've been preparing for. You go get 'em, Joey."

"I'll do that, Mom."

"Now where's your black T-shirt?" She sniffled.

Sleep didn't come easily that night. I wrestled with angels and expectations, and awoke unscathed. My dad knocked on my door and poked his head in.

"Well who's ready for his last Connecticut breakfast? "

He had a wide, gleaming smile that made everything seem so wonderful.

"Yeah, I'm totally ready, Dad." I tore out of the bedroom and into the kitchen, towards the smell of French toast cooking.

"So are you excited about being a real New Yorker?"

He placed the French toast on my plate with an unusually large serving of syrup.

"Yeah, Dad! I can't believe I'll be on my own and everything. I'm a little worried about the kids in my new school, though. It's tough coming in mid year."

"I don't think they'll give you too much trouble. You're used to being viewed as a bit of an outsider. It never bothered you before. Maybe Grandma will be right, maybe they'll be a little more sophisticated and artsy than the average kid around here."

"Yeah, I hope so."

I filled up my bowl with Corn Chex and Reeses

Puffs.

"Pass the milk, Dad, please."

"So Uncle Mischa is really looking forward to meeting you, I understand. Boy, are you going to have a great "study buddy" in him. He'll really help move your practices along."

"Mom said he's really demanding. Do you think he'll yell?"

"I don't know. He's a teacher; he's used to having to be patient, and more importantly, he's a world class violinist. You couldn't pay to have someone like that as your daily mentor, you know?"

So, I finished breakfast, then we swung by Grandma's house, picked her up, and before I knew it, I was boarding Metro North to Grand Central Station. I hugged and kissed my grandma, mom, and dad as if I would never see them again—even though it was just for the semester.

Grandma's eyes welled up just a little, but she obviously felt this was the right thing for me to be doing now, because she had this look of "Grandma determination" on her face. I can't quite explain what that is, it was more the way the corners of her eyes squinted together, enunciating wrinkles under the folds of her lower lids. They were the loves and wars of her 82 years. I blew her one last kiss as I headed through gate 17. Mom and Dad squeezed me tightly and told me to call every night. Dad gave me the thumbs up. Mom looked away. Take one step at a time, I thought to myself. Don't think about everything that lies ahead, you'll drown!

I found my seat—two across. I had the window, and that was a nice start. I put my bag in the overhead rack, then my violin. I draped my windbreaker over the top of the violin case, which made me feel as though it was being taken care of. I took my seat and stared out the window. Wow, this was exciting.

A few minutes later a kid around my age sat down next to me in the aisle seat. He had a small black bag that he stuffed under the seat in front of him, and a new VAIO. As soon as he settled in, he placed the computer on his lap. In moments, he was typing away. I tried not to be troublesome by making small talk, but we were traveling for almost an hour and I was getting a little "oochy." Actually, I was going out of my mind. I had to peak at what he was typing. I leaned back in my seat to catch a glimpse. *What could he be working on so industriously,* I thought? A letter to a friend, a homework assignment? . . . It didn't look like that to me? I had to see.

There was one long paragraph which he obviously had been editing over and over during this whole time:

"I waited until I saw the sun turn pink then plum . . . no, lavender and hues of indigo, burnt umber, luscious, languorous, all at once fire and fury, then sobering my senses, cobalt and periwinkle, deeply calming yet disrupting. I felt strangely moved by it— all the way up the beach, in fact. It was so big to me when I was five. As I walked I felt it gently swallowing me, covering me with the hot velvet of an old blanket, bigger and bigger till it could possess all of who I was—own me, embrace me, when no one else could."

He caught me.

"I'm writing a short story for a magazine. I'm a writer," he said, startling me.

"Oh, I'm sorry for being nosey. It's my first time on

a train and I was just observing everything, I guess."

"That's good, to observe. It's the whole process behind writing," He hesitated for a minute. "At least that's what I've heard. My father is a writer. I've been trying to get something published since I was 11. I'm 14 now. It's hard, you know?"

"My name's Joey," I could tell he was way too involved in his process to introduce himself. He was also way too involved in his adjectives to make his point clear to a reader. But I didn't know him well enough yet to comment on his writing technique.

"Oh, I'm Greg. Are you from Connecticut?"

"Yeah, born and bred."

"Me too," he added. "I'm trying to write for this local magazine, and I'm supposed to write what I know, but I don't know that much 'cause I've never been anywhere, done anything. So what am I supposed to write?" He shifted uncomfortably in his seat, his foot hadn't stopped tapping since he told me his name.

"So, for my birthday this year. My parents are sending me to New York City for the semester. I'm taking a semester off from high school and I'm going to live like a real writer. I'll be staying with my older sister who is a painter. She's doing really well too . . . exhibiting a lot, selling some."

"Does she have her own place in town?" I asked.

"Sort of. She shares a loft with another girl and a guy in NOHO."

"Noho? I've heard of Soho, but what's with the 'no.'?"

"Ha!" He liked that. "That's where you live in Manhattan when you can't pay the rent in Soho!"

We both had a good laugh.

"Anyway, I expect lots of things to happen to me in the city, and if I can't write my story, I'll write somebody else's." It really appeared that he had worked this all out before he ever verbalized it to me.

"That sounds like a plan," I said somewhat noncommittally. This idea of writing someone else's life just seemed so foreign to me. Why would you be interested? It's hard enough figuring out your own life!

"I like your descriptions of the sun," I remarked, trying to keep the conversation going.

"Thanks, but it's really a symbolic description of how I felt about my life at five. My dad traveled a lot because of his novels. He was always collecting data, experiences, other people's lives. That didn't give him a whole lot of time for mine. You know what I mean?"

Greg said that a lot, "You know what I mean?" He must not have had many people in his life who understood him.

"I guess I didn't feel very secure, so I looked to my environment instead of the people in it, to make me feel that way, you know what I mean?"

"Yes, I get that," I nodded.

"We're all ultimately just trying to figure out what fills us up?"

"I guess so," I said. I had never thought about life in those terms before. Frankly, I just thought it was a series of random occurrences linked together by lots of "practice."

"So, what fills you up? How old are you anyway?"

"Music," I answered, "and I'm thirteen."

"What are you going to New York for?"

"To do my music," I continued.

"Wow! You've found it already at thirteen. You're so lucky. Most kids are still running after a soccer ball at that age. And that's okay, you know. They just get to the big questions later in life than we do."

I liked being accepted as a deep thinker like Greg was, but somehow it didn't ring true for me.

"To be honest with you, I didn't realize I was dealing with any big questions. I'm just doin' what comes naturally."

"Yeah, but it's not all natural. You study and work at your music a lot, don't you? Are you going to New York to study or to do it?"

"Both," I said. "I'm a violinist. I'm going to live with my uncle, who is also a violinist, and attend The American Institute of Music. I'll study there, go to middle school in the neighborhood, and, if I'm lucky, get a few solo performances on the side. So I expect to be studying and doing," I accented my last word. After all, I was a doer!

"Well, it can't be both. You either take this time to study and progress, or you go and do and perform and experience music, which means you have to experience life!"

"I experience life," I retorted, a little hurt by the notion that Greg "lived" more than I do.

"But you have never been totally free! You have your chance now. This semester . . . this year. Listen, I'm gonna' give you my phone number. Whenever you feel like hitting the town, going out, getting a little crazy, call me. I'm your man. It's good for me. I need experiences."

"Yeah, sure," I said, unconvinced. He needs experiences, even if they're not his. I was off to make my own experiences. I took his number anyway and stuffed it into my pocket. Maybe it would fall out, maybe not. Maybe it was good to know someone else in the city beside my uncle. Who knows what he'd be like?

CHAPTER 5

GHOSTS FROM THE PAST

When I stopped talking long enough to think, I began to remember all that had transpired in my small life the past few months; it was staggering. I had to review it. I had to visit the past before it escaped my thirteen year old consciousness and became buried in the comfort of memory's convenient nest. I thought about the months that took my zayde's life, and simultaneously propelled me into the music spotlight. It was a time of great sadness. It was a time of provisional joy. I should revisit them now, on this train bound for my future. I turned my head toward the window and watched the pictures of my past flash through the pane. I saw November 2002, before Zayde died.

Every Saturday, late afternoon, I used to bring my violin and overnight bag to Grandma and Zayde's house after conservatory. They lived right around the block from me. Their house had beige shingles, stone, and a big picture window in the front where the living room was. The garden was planted with an odd but pleasing combination of yuccas, weeping spruce, and impatiens. A large boulder with earthy striations sat imposingly in the front. I had claimed it as mine when I was three. I used to stand on it and announce my grandeur every time I came to visit. It was an inviting house.

So I'd ring the doorbell and Zayde would come running.

"Okay, okay, that's my boy there—my Joey."

"Yep, it's me, Zayde," I'd call through the door.

The door would fly open and there he was, robust cheeks, round face, mostly bald, laughing hazel eyes, and suspenders. Always suspenders. My grandfather had battled pancreatic cancer four years before, and had never regained much of his weight. He went through the eight hour Whipple Procedure, where they cut out much of your stomach and intestines and leave you with just enough to survive. I guess they don't figure you'll be surviving too long with that anyway. But Zayde did. He beat all the odds and was now in his 4th year, cancer free. Everyday was such a celebration. And every Saturday at 5:00 P.M. he waited for me to tell him all about my day at conservatory.

Grandma would make some tea with honey, and we'd all sit in the den. I'd cuddle up between the two of them and go through the details. My grandfather wanted to know every piece I played, what new anecdotes Mr. Herrington told, what new stories I had about the kids, and most importantly, how I played in performance class. When I told him how pleased my teacher was, and how respected my work was by my peers, his face just shone with pride. He'd give a little zayde laugh and say, "Ah, that's my boy. My Joey." For me, no performance or Saturday was complete without a debriefing by Zayde.

His name was Gershon Levinson and he never played an instrument. He was a CPA—certified public accountant. He never missed a single concert or small performance that I did, since I started violin at three years of age. He didn't care if I was playing with orchestra or as a soloist, if I was playing *Twinkle Twinkle* or the *Bruch Violin Concerto*. Nothing was too hard for him to get to, when it concerned his grandson.

He had a beautiful, mellow baritone voice, and could pick out any tune on the piano. He loved that. Always with one hand and two fingers. He just got such a kick out of the fact that his grandson, the child that his daughter made, was a violin prodigy. "How did I get so lucky?" He'd remark.

"It's gotta' be in the genes," I'd say.

"Nah, you've begun your own line with this. Imagine your children. Oy, I should only be here to see them."

Well, that was not meant to be.

In November of 2002, Zayde's luck ran out. He wasn't able to eat for days, and was getting swollen around his stomach. He came to a concert I played at the Jewish Museum in Manhattan, but he could hardly walk. I played the Bloch Nigun and he began to cry. I had never seen Zayde cry. I never saw it again. Something was very wrong.

The next day he went to the doctor. They took a CAT scan. It was back. The cancer was back. My grandma was crying on the phone, the whole family spoke in whispers. It had spread. The doctor gave Zayde six months.

I came home every day from school and called Zayde. He always sounded upbeat, asking about my grades, my practice. I always told him the day's events, and asked how he felt. His response became part of our ritual, "Exactly the way I'm supposed to feel, Joey. Just that way." I never probed any further.

One week later, he began chemo. It did not go well. My mom wouldn't let me see Zayde that week. She said he was sleeping all the time. I heard her tell Dad that Zayde looked like death. I saw him one week later, he was only a shadow of what I remembered.

I kept thinking, this doesn't look like six months to me. He's aged ten years in one week.

The next week Zayde went back to the doctor. I called him after school but he wouldn't come to the phone. Grandma said he had to rest and Mom said he was just a little sad.

"He's going to die sooner, isn't he?" I asked.

"Three months," Mom said. This was the end of November.

I went about my business. I had a concert at Carnegie Recital Hall scheduled for the second week in December, right before the December school break. I rehearsed furiously with my accompanist, Luba. Luba was my comfort during all performances and rehearsals. She was round and Russian, with a pretty face, red cheeks, and sparkling blue eyes that danced when she liked the way I played. Her hair was reddish blonde and sat puffed up high on her head. She was soft spoken and enjoyed teaching me new words in Russian each time she came, which was every week.

I had quite a collection of stuffed animals, bears, dogs, cats, snakes, mice, and I would set a different one on the piano every time I rehearsed. I often brought out the white mouse because Luba got such a kick out of it. It was a puppet, and if her hands were cold when she arrived at my house, she'd slip him on her right hand to warm up. She called him Muwishka.

"Mishka?" I'd say

"No, muwishka," she'd correct, mishka is a bear."

I was thrilled to be playing Sarasate's *Zigeunerweisen* and the 3rd movement of the Bruch *Violin Concerto in G minor* for this concert, along with the Bloch *Nigun* (which was in repertoire already), a Chopin *Nocturne* and Gershwin's, *It Ain't Necessarily So.* Almost all new pieces. I played Carnegie Recital Hall every year and it was a very big deal for me. I always had to get psychologically prepared to walk out onto that stage and give 'em hell! Well, you know what I mean.

In between rehearsals and practice and lessons I went to school as usual. How come every time I had a concert, the tests and project assignments got heavier? During the week of Carnegie, I had three tests and an English project due, along with three hours a day of practice, two two-hour lessons, and two accompanist rehearsals. Enough to kill the Terminator! But I plodded along. Mom kept me organized, made sure I got to sleep before 10:00 P.M. each night, and kept me from losing my temper on numerous occasions. I didn't speak to Zayde all week. I missed him, but was afraid of what I would hear in his voice. I couldn't deal with it. Better shut it out. Gotta' keep up for performance.

The night before Carnegie, Zayde called.

"Hey, how's my guy? I didn't want to bother you this week, but now I'll bother you. How do you feel? Ready to knock'em dead?"

His voice was very low but it still sounded like Zayde.

"Yeah Zaydl, I'm psyched! Will you be there?"

"You know, Joey, I've never missed a performance, but I can't walk . . . well, if someone lifts me I can move slowly with a walker but I'd be an awful nuisance at Carnegie Hall. It's a little dangerous for me to be out like that, you know? But you call me the minute you get home, I'll be up and waiting to hear, okay?"

I could tell his voice was quivering. He was holding back tears. In the thirteen years that I was on this earth, he never missed a moment in my life that was important. He drove me to lessons when they were scheduled in the city at nights and Mom was working, he came to accompanist rehearsals when I needed an audience to practice for, he was there at every birthday, when I took my first steps, said my first words, and scratched on my first 16th size violin—smaller than a toy."

I remembered, as I spoke to him, that last year, Ms. Liebling had wanted me to have an accompanist rehearsal at her home with Luba the day before another major concert. My teacher always insisted that she hear the whole program with accompanist, immediately prior to the concert, even if she had heard it a month earlier.

"Things change, schatsy" she would say. "Rhythm gets sloppy, dynamics get forgotten, fingerings get concocted!"

Of course she was right. There was nothing that made you feel better than completing your whole concert program with your teacher the day before. So I had to go. The only problem was that my mom was on deadline for a magazine article, and couldn't leave the house till she put it in the mail. Anyway, I didn't know how I would get to my teacher's house in Short Hills, New Jersey. I called Zayde and told him my tale of woe.

"Don't you worry, Joey, I'll cancel my clients for tomorrow afternoon and take you myself. How's that?"

"Oh Zayde, you will? I can't believe it. You're the best."

"Sure, no problem. How hard can it be to get to Short Hills?"

The next day, three hours into what should have been a two hour trip, and a few wrong turns later, we pulled up to my teacher's house. The map to New Jersey still lay on my lap, turned inside out, and in general disorder. But we got there. Such a Zayde!

But now he wouldn't be at Carnegie and I'd miss him. There would be an undeniable hole in the audience, and nothing I could do to fix it. I hung up the phone with him and felt the void.

Saturday came. I didn't attend conservatory that day because I'd be totally burnt out for the concert. I slept late, had a great practice with my mom and just read for a while. By 4:00 P.M. I was ready to perform! I took a shower. Mom did my hair—gel, blow drying, the works. I slipped on my shirt, tuxedo, and bow tie. I had to rehearse in them before the performance. You always have to be sure you're totally comfortable.

Sure enough, as I played, my bow kept snagging on the button of my tuxedo. Mom said that I must have grown and the angle wasn't right between my bow and buttons anymore. Better play without the jacket. Come out in it and bow, then take it off at the piano and tune up the violin. The audience would understand and even think it was a dramatic touch. Okay, it was decided—no jacket.

I went to my computer after rehearsal to check messages. I always felt so good to see my friends from conservatory leaving me messages of good luck before a really important concert. Kids in regular school didn't really "get it," what I was all about, but friends at A.I.M. understood how monumental a concert at Carnegie Recital Hall was.

It's funny. It's just a place—a place with a stage where you get up and make your music. But it has such a powerful ghost. You feel him when you step out under the chandelier and look forward. He hangs from the balcony I think. You can only feel him there if you're performing. He's friendly and all encompassing. He reminds you immediately you're part of a legacy—a spiritual place whose walls enfold years and years of the greatest music ever made—by the greatest musicians who ever lived. He doesn't make me nervous. He makes me proud. Anyway, there were the messages—7,8, 9 in total. "Knock 'em dead Joey," "Be awesome, Joey," "We can't wait to hear about it, Joey."

Okay, I was ready to do it. My family— Mom, Dad and Grandma, loaded into my dad's ML, and we began the pensive ride into the city. It's funny when I look back at my years of concerts, some rides were light hearted, filled with conversation and anecdotes, others were consistently quiet and thoughtful. The ride to Carnegie was always like that. It was a pilgrimage—a spiritual preparation. Some non-specific classical music would be playing on the radio, and no one would speak. My mom always said she'd hold her breath from the time we entered the car to the time I took my final bows. That's my mom!

Once I arrived I felt much better. There was Luba, smiling and excited."You are ready Joey, yes? You'll play your very best tonight, I know."

I beamed up at her, not wanting to disappoint. I saw the stage manager, Tom. He was a nice guy, tall as a string bean with wire rimmed glasses, a face as long as he was tall, and a ready handshake.

"Hey young man, good to have you back. I hear we're gonna' have some media in the audience tonight. Better be good!" He laughed.

"Oh wow, really?" I asked. I wasn't sure whether to be nervous or psyched. I guess a little of both was in order.

"I'll try my best," I added. I always had a soft spot for Tom because the first time I ever played Carnegie Recital Hall, three years earlier, I asked Tom if he could possibly take me onto main stage Carnegie after my concert was over. The concerts at Carnegie Recital (an exact replica of Carnegie Hall, but in miniature), and Stern Hall (the big one), ended at the same time. He said he would.

At the end of my concert, three and a half years ago, before I went out to the reception to greet everyone, Tom grabbed me and said, "Well, now's your chance. Follow me and bring that golden violin of yours."

I grabbed Mergatroyd (as I lovingly called my ½ size violin), and entered the back elevator. The doors opened and we walked backstage through a winding corridor. Suddenly we emerged from the wings onto the stage.

"Oh my. I can't believe I'm here." I'm sure if I had thought about it a minute longer I'd have been trembling, but I didn't tremble. I picked up Mergatroyd and began to play. . . . Variations on a Theme by Corelli. I was 9 years old and I was playing my ½ size violin on the great stage of Carnegie Hall (Stern Hall). Members of the Cleveland Orchestra were in the process of packing up from their concert that night. They stopped to listen to me. I knew it too, but I wasn't nervous. I was loving it. This was a dream—a wonderful, wonderful dream—Oh please don't wake me.

As I played, I looked. I saw everything. The masterful carvings, the gently curved balconies, the chandelier . . . the ghosts . . . oh the ghosts were absolutely palpable. I couldn't believe how my little violin played in these walls. It was as if the bow was pulling itself, because I certainly wasn't. I was too busy feeling the past. My fingers flew across the finger board tickling the positions, and I felt them. I felt them all inside me, in front of me, surrounding me . . . Heifetz, Oistrakh, Menuhin, Rabin, Stern, Zuckerman, Perlman. How did I get so lucky? I didn't belong here. . . . I didn't care. A boy has to dream. So I dreamed, and while I dreamed I knew that I'd be back some day, and the house would be full.

I finished and I heard applause coming from behind me. It was members of the first violin section from Cleveland.

"Hey, you're somethin' else," one said

"Make sure you send a tape to the Cleveland Orchestra next year. You should definitely come solo with us," added the next.

"Thanks," I said, totally entranced.

"Okay young fella'," said Tom, "Time to go."

I left but I've never forgotten.

I shook off my wonderful memory and got back to concentrating on the present in Carnegie Recital Hall. I tuned up with Luba, ran some passages of my pieces and went off stage to relax and let the hall fill up. Some of my friends from conservatory ran back to see me.

Catherine came back and calmed me by telling stories from the day's orchestra rehearsal.

"Oh you should'a heard Herrington today. He kept railing on about how the first violins couldn't keep it together without Joey there. He said we were sluggish. That we had been eating too much cafeteria food. Can you believe that? The nerve. I was playing a hundred miles an hour. Sluggish my foot!"

I laughed at how peeved Catherine was. Herrington did that whenever either violinist from the first two stands was missing at an orchestra rehearsal. He tried to rile up the masses. It usually worked.

"I swear, you'd think he'd give us better images to work with, too. We were doing the Rimsky Korsakov and he says, 'Play it like your monks. That's right . . . be a bunch of monks.' What kind of imagery is that? How do we know what a bunch of monks sound like? Really!"

Whoa, Catherine was on the war path. It sounded like it was a really funny session. I kinda' wished I had been there. That's the thing with the Saturday Pre-College Conservatory Program, you curse having to get up in the morning for it, but within minutes of not being there, you miss it terribly.

I told Catherine I'd see her after the concert and she could complain to me some more. She left. I was alone. So alone I could hear my own breath. I waited.

The stage manager knocked on my door.

"Three minutes Joey. You ready?"

"You bet," I said.

The house lights flickered and went off. Then came the announcement about turning off cell phones, and not using flash photography. The audience applauded. I was on. I didn't even feel my feet move. How'd I get out there? The house was packed. I bowed deeply, removed my jacket, and walked over to the piano to tune. One day I'd be tuning in front of an orchestra, I thought to myself. I walked to the appointed spot on the stage, placed my bow, nodded to Luba and we were off.

All the pieces went off without a hitch. I was so worried about forgetting one of the repeats in the *Zigeunerweisen*, but I made it. It felt good. I'd get a debriefing from my mom and Ms. Liebling later, no doubt, but for now I glowed in the reception of a standing, roaring crowd. I guess they liked it. It was the first time Zayde wasn't out there. There was that hole. I bowed numerous times, accepted flowers from various admirers, the house continued to roar. It was almost enough—this thirteen year old man/child in a far too fine tuxedo, standing on the stage at Carnegie Recital Hall, accepting the ultimate nod for his years of sacrifice. It was almost enough—this wave of affirmation that I had disturbed many molecules in the audience tonight. I had always heard that expression, "a musician's job is to disturb the molecules in his audience." No one should ever leave the concert hall feeling the same way they had when they entered. They must be changed by the experience. I had achieved that. It was almost enough. I left the stage and collapsed in a thirteen year old heap in the green room. My teacher came running backstage.

"Ah, schatsy, schatsy you were amazing! A miracle! So musical! So many good things, Joey. I'm proud of you."

There was nothing quite like knowing that I made my teacher proud. It is something I can't explain. Nobody can understand it unless they live this life. When Ms. Liebling was wowed, I knew life would be grand, at least for the next month. She could live off that pride for many weeks, which meant Joey was a happy boy for many weeks. You know, the pedagogues at this level are so tough and so demanding, there is no difference between you at thirteen or another student at eighteen with a full time, traveling solo career. You are treated the same, and the same is expected of you. It can get a little tough to take. But as I said, this was a good night. My teacher was proud. The audience was happy. My parents were, no doubt, beaming, and I didn't have any middle school tests to wake up and study for the next day.

Friends from pre-college were pushing through the crowds forming at the inner backstage door. I walked out and met everyone. It was both a thrilling and uneasy part of the whole process. Now, for the next half hour, I was smiling and hugging and saying thank you, to people, in many cases, I'd never met. This time there were a few with cameras and pads. I hadn't noticed that before. I wondered who they were and where they were from, but I figured if they wanted me to know they'd tell me.

The next day, Sunday, I called Zayde. His speech sounded a little slurred and his voice was low again, but he still sounded like Zayde. I told him every detail. I wanted him to feel as though he had been there. I told him I was looking forward to the Channukah dinner Mom was making at the end of the next week. He said he was too. He sounded sad. I tried to block it out.

CHAPTER 6

FIFTEEN MINUTES OF FAME

Monday at 11:36 A.M. my mom came to call for me at school, which was the usual time, and she was all excited.

"Joey, there was a wonderful young conductor at Carnegie on Saturday night, named Gabriel Chance. He is the conductor of the Metropolitan Chamber Symphony. He heard you and he wants you to audition for the spot of soloist with his orchestra, playing The Bruch Violin Concerto in G minor at Lincoln Center this October 22nd. Can you believe that? It's a good thing you have the Bruch in repertoire.

"Wow, a chance to play as the soloist with orchestra. Mom, I was dreaming about that at the concert this weekend. I was dreaming about when I'd solo with orchestra. I never thought it would be this soon."

I had never performed with orchestra before. I mean, you know, I had been first violin and even concert master of orchestras before, but those were orchestras at pre-college. I had never been featured as the soloist with a professional orchestra behind me. What an honor. What a dream. I better get to work.

So, I came home, called the conductor and made a date for the end of the week. I'd be ready by then. I practiced for hours over the next few days, Bruch, Bruch, and nothing but the Bruch!

Friday morning came, and Mom and Dad drove me into the city. This was big. I took the elevator up to the 25th floor, got off, walked to the left and there was a large door with a highly polished brass knob. I looked around, it was the only entrance door on the floor. Whoa, this is gonna' be a cool apartment. I rang the bell; Mom was behind me, Dad waited double-parked downstairs. You could die waiting for a parking space in Manhattan.

A medium-sized man with an over-sized voice answered the door. It was Maestro Chance. He invited us in with a booming baritone. "Well, well, Josef, it's good to meet you in person. I heard you play at Carnegie. You knocked everybody's socks off. I can't wait to hear your Bruch.

"Thank you. I'm looking forward to playing it for you." I was so excited, I couldn't even hear my own voice. It was an out of body experience.

"Okay, then, let's get right to it." We walked into the living room. There were three other gentlemen sitting on the beautifully upholstered sofas. (In an apartment like that, you need to say sofas—couches sound so gauche.)

"Let me introduce you to three of my first violinists: Jonathan Marks, Anton Shenkoff, and Viktor Germanhoff." (He was German!) We all shook hands and did our requisite "pleasure to meet yous" and then I walked to the piano. I quickly opened my violin case, put on my chin pad, rosined up the bow and tuned. I was ready.

I began the first movement and I let the music take

me. I had this feeling of mastery sweep over me as I remembered first learning the Bruch the year before. Ms. Liebling always believed you should perform a concerto for as many months as possible, then put it away; so the next time you take it out to play (perhaps six months or a year later), you're a more seasoned player, and all the technical points that were once difficult are easy now. She was right. Everything certainly sounded different now than it had a year earlier. I felt more in control, more able to express the composer's dynamics. More directed. Before I knew it, I was in the middle of the second movement. I love that slow movement. A lot of slow 2nd movements are boring and uninteresting, not just for the audience, but for the artist as well. I guess they're just harder to write. But the Bruch 2nd movement sings. I played about a page and the conductor stopped me and asked me to play some of the third movement. I was hoping that was a good sign.

They allowed me to finish the third movement, then they broke into applause.

"Bravo, Josef. Fantastic! Beautiful! Give us a few seconds, will you? Wait in the hall way."

I went to join my mom in the hall, and we waited for five interminable minutes. A lot goes through your mind in five minutes. I was receiving a déjà vu from my American Institute of Music audition. I was nine years old. I played a movement from Haydn's *Concerto in C Major* and Dvorak's *Slavonic Dance*. It was the first time in my life that I remember being truly nervous. I mean . . . rattled. So rattled that I began playing the first movement without my accompanist. I just left her behind, then I looked at her after the first line as if to say, "So where were you?"

Poor Luba. She didn't seem to mind though, she knew I was a wreck. After all, you walk into an audition room with ten judgmental pedagogues all looking for a reason not to accept you, all trying to find something wrong so one can look more knowledgeable than another—that's hard on a kid. I know now that not all of them are like this, but many are. There is no reason for them to take you over someone else unless you blow them away. They don't know how good natured, kind, hard working, or devoted you are. They don't know anything about you. You have to tell them your life's story in 10 minutes of performing. Your talent does the talking. No room for mistakes.

I knew I played really well, but I didn't know if they would think my early start in the Haydn was unprofessional, and then not accept me. As I mentioned earlier, age is never the consideration in the music world. It's how professional and prodigious you can sound.

So I waited. It was maybe three or four minutes before someone came out. He was a kind looking man. The only one, beside Ms. Liebling, who had a smile on his face from the moment I walked in. I certainly made a mental note of that. He introduced himself.

"Hey Josef, my name is Professor Krantz. I just wanted to tell you that your results will be in by the end of next week. You'll get a letter, but I can call you if you'd like. I thought you were superb. What a wonderful, deep sound you have—great musicality, and imaginative musical ideas. I like that. I believe the rest of the faculty felt the same way.

"Thank you so much. Yes, would you really call me

next week to let me know?"

I couldn't believe how nice he was being. Of course, he did call me, I did get in, and Professor Krantz wound up being one of my violin coaches—specializing in musical ideas and orchestral score reading. Ms. Liebling was my teacher of technique. I loved them both. She was intense and devoted, it was always evident how much she cared for me and I for her; he was a breath of fresh air, a fun-loving, supremely artistic music-maker, amidst all the life and death seriousness of the institution. Such memories. They seemed as though they existed with me in a totally other reality.

Maestro Chance called me in. It stunned me back to reality. I walked into the living room feeling refreshed from my journey of memory.

"Josef, we have listened to lots of young prodigies for this Lincoln Center engagement, but we are all in complete agreement that you should get this performance opportunity. You are the real thing. Congratulations."

My face turned bright red, I'm sure. I could feel the heat, my heart pumping, my smile uncontrollable, my voice felt as if it was emerging from someone else's body.

"Oh thank you so much. Thank you. Thank you."

"Now Josef, as you work on readying the third movement for us, I'd like you to concentrate on the rhythmic pulse of the opening. It should be crisp like 'Yum, digga-dum, Bum Bum, digga-dum.' And then for the next part, you should keep in your ear this kind of feeling . . . 'deeeeya dada, deeeeya dada.'"

He turned to his concert master, "Right? Don't you

think, Jonathan?"

"Oh definitely 'deeeeya dada,'—without question."

"Yes, well then, it's settled," proclaimed Maestro Chance, and he laughed the deepest most resonant laugh I've ever heard.

"You got that Josef?" He asked with a self satisfied smile.

"Oh yes sir, 'deeeyadada' it will be! I repeated joyfully. "I can't wait for rehearsals! Thanks again, soooo much."

"You earned it, Josef. We'll be in touch in a couple of months to begin work. The concert is next October 22nd." He ushered me out of the parlor and into the hall.

I had done it. Not only did I have an orchestral debut—but one at Lincoln Center. This was a dream. I had to call Zayde. I had to instant message Catherine. I had to call my teachers. Ms. Liebling and Professor Krantz would flip!

CHAPTER 7

FROM THE SUBLIME TO THE . . .

The next morning was school. I think I spent the whole day dreaming of my debut which now adorned my future like a string of pearls. I was seated in my usual blue chair in the principal's office at 11:36 A.M., waiting for my mom to pick me up. The day's musical endeavors were about to begin.

Sitting next to me was a student with more dubious reasons for being in the office. His name was Stu. Stu was a big kid with a short haircut. He had one of those flips—it's kind of a fad these days—where the hair is kept almost like a crew cut but it has this slope of hair that points up in the front. That part is usually dyed blond. So was Stu's. I'd express my opinion of this style but, frankly, I'm afraid it will get back to STU!

Anyway, there I sat, looking at the walls, thinking of all the homework that was facing me after the hours of practice ahead when suddenly he spoke.

"Yo man, you goin' home?"

"Yeah," I said carefully, not wanting to arouse any unforeseen aggression.

"You are so lucky, man. We all have to stay in this hole for three more hours."

"Well, lucky isn't exactly how I would put it. It's

just what I do. What classes do you have left this afternoon?"

"Ummm, lunch, recess . . ." (big pause, you could tell Stu was really straining himself), "gym, typing, and health."

"Well, those sound like fun classes to me. They're a vacation compared to what I'll be doing. I'm not just going home and relaxing, you know."

"Well, what do ya have to do?"

"From here I either eat my lunch in the car on the way into the city, and have a two hour violin lesson, or I go straight to an accompanist rehearsal, or I have a quick lunch and continue the other two hours of my practice that I didn't get to in the morning. I only have time for an hour's practice in the morning."

"That's sick, man. You need to get out more!"

"I've heard that before."

"Yeah, you should come party with me and my friends on Saturday. We go to the park, set off some fireworks, walk to Starbucks, have coffee and chill and stuff."

"Ummm, that sounds great, but you know . . . I'm in the city doing music on Saturdays. It's not fireworks, but it's pretty good. Thanks for the invite, though."

At that moment my mom pulled up. Not a minute too soon. Not that I didn't enjoy discussing the virtues of purchasing illegal fireworks or drinking Venti Mocha Lattes, but Ms. Liebling's studio was looking pretty good right now.

I signed out and hopped into Mom's car. The signs of a two hour violin lesson were next to me on the seat: A brown bag with an "everything bagel" and orange juice, my green music bag filled with etude and exercise books, rosin and orchestral scores, and of course, Rowena, my ¾ sized violin. It was such a beauty—a dark, warm sound on the low strings and a sweet E string. A big sound too, that could really do justice in a concert hall. Even the color of the wood was dark. It looked old, and in the violin business, that was a good thing. The older your violin (if, of course it was a good one), the more valuable it was. We had just bought her, and I was a very proud owner. This was a valuable way to spend an afternoon, I thought.

Mom and I made pleasant conversation.

"So anything exciting in school today? Classes all good?"

"Sure. Classes are always good." I really felt that way most of the time, too. I enjoyed my mornings at middle school. I felt independent, responsible and very appreciated. My teachers were extremely nice people, and good educators on top of it. That's always helpful.

"In math we had assessment tests and tomorrow we're having more assessment tests, and on Friday, we'll have science assessment tests."

My mom laughed. "My, Joey, when do they have time to teach you enough material to be assessed on if there are always assessment tests? I had calls from two newspapers today, *The Daily News* and *Newsday*. You won't believe this . . . they want to do stories on you. It seems there were a few reporters in the audience at Carnegie Saturday. You sure did it this time, honey!"

I was over the moon. "So what do I have to do? Are

they going to interview me?"

"Yes. *Newsday* is coming today, and the *Daily News Reporter* will come tomorrow—both at 12:00 P.M. What do ya think of that?"

I couldn't believe my luck. That's a career making move, getting interviewed by the city and borough papers. We pulled into our driveway and my feet didn't even touch the ground. I ran into my room, changed clothes, and washed up just in time for the bell to ring. My mom and I went to the door together. I opened it and in walked two women—a young woman with long brown hair, smartly dressed in a navy suit and pumps, and a middle-aged woman with wire-frame glasses, long wild blonde hair, wearing jeans and a denim shirt and carrying a large camera.

"Well, I remember you from Carnegie Recital Hall. You are quite a talented young man. My name is Moira Richards. I'm with *Newsday,* and this is one of our wonderful photographers, Joyce Peterson."

"A pleasure to meet you," I responded. My mom shook hands and continued with the pleasantries of offering them each something to drink and a comfortable place to sit in our den. Ms. Peterson snapped photos for the first ½ hour of my interview. Some were candids, and some she asked me to pose for with my violin. Then she left. Ms. Richards continued to ask me questions for the next 1 ½ hours. Luckily I wasn't shy. I loved an audience in any form, so I gave her anecdotes and serious commentary about my life as a young, professional musician.

When the interview was over, Moira, as she now had me call her, assured me that her article would be in next week's weekend edition, and she left.

The next day I did the same dance with the reporter from *The Daily News.* He was a man about 6'5", dressed in a navy blazer, and gold and navy striped tie. What was it with these reporters and navy blue? Any way he had black hair and friendly, round brown eyes. He said his name was Bill. Bill came alone for the interview and explained that his photographer would follow the next day and snap photos for about an hour's session. Wow, the bigger the paper, the longer the sessions are. And in fact, that was true, because he interviewed me for two hours. It was still fun though.

I was getting better and better at it. You know, questions like, "Did I want to make music my life? When did I start? Who were my greatest influences? Describe my teacher's methods. How much do I practice every day? Favorite solo artists and why? My ultimate goal as a soloist? What is the field like for a thirteen year old? Does my practice and performance schedule get in the way of my social life? Do I have friends?"

"Do I have friends?" What do you think? You become serious about an area of study at a young age and you automatically lose your friends? Now that was a ridiculous question. A better question would have been: "Do you think your friends understand you?" or "What do your friends think of your life style at this age?" But, "Do you have friends?" It is so typical for an outsider to assume prodigious kids are totally a-social.

Well anyway, I told him my friends are mostly conservatory kids, who understand my routine because they do it too. I had some friends from public school who I thought were pretty special people, and who respected what I was into, but there weren't too many in that category. The truth was that Southbury Middle School kids on the whole, didn't understand where I was coming from. I just had certain dreams that didn't include a whole lot of unstructured free time; my conservatory friends and I shared a different reality. I could talk to them and not be judged for what I did and who I was. I just couldn't get into this whole concept with Bill, though. He was a reporter, not a musician—I didn't feel like making the story about my differences—it was about my music.

So Bill left with a handshake and a promise that his article would come out the following Monday. What a media blitz that would be: *Newsday* out on the weekend and *The Daily News* out on Monday! The next day, as Bill promised, his photographer came and took photos for the entire hour of my accompanist rehearsal at home. He took me from every angle (I mean, he was at every angle, I was just standing and playing): sitting on the floor, sitting on a chair, sitting on the stairs, leaning against the railing, leaning on the piano, leaning on his belly on the floor, looking up (a strange shot, I would think). All this time, I was running through my pieces with Luba. She didn't know what to make of all this. She just kept playing and smiling, and I did what I had to do. At the end of the hour, the photographer left. I was relieved.

Sunday morning came and we rushed out to the nearest newsstand to pick up *Newsday*. We opened to the Human Interest section and there it was. A full page, with a color photo. It was my first major newspaper coverage. The phones did not stop ringing all day. Friends, families, teachers. It was so cool. My mom said this was just the beginning. She was right.

Monday at 11:36 A.M. Mom came to pick me up again. She had a huge smile on her face and looked like she was bursting to tell me something.

"Joey," she chirped "you won't believe who I was on the phone with all morning."

"Okay, who? Tell me!"

"A segment producer from *Good Morning America,* and a segment producer from *The Letterman Show.* Your article came out in *The Daily News* this morning, and the news and talk shows are all over it. They want you to appear on their shows this week.

"What? Are you kidding? What are they saying?"

"They seem to think you're the up and coming young star in the classical music industry. I certainly wasn't going to argue with them. You're a star to us!" She laughed whole heartedly. My mom did everything whole heartedly, she believed life was too short to do anything with half a heart.

"So when do they want me?"

"Well, *GMA* called first thing this morning, asked a lot of questions and said they'd get back to me later in the morning with a date. One hour later, *Letterman*'s show called, and asked if they could be the first TV show appearance you'd make. I said we'd like to comply but *GMA* did call first and if they call back with a date first, we'll have to honor that. *The Letterman* people said they'd get working on it at once. So that's where we stand now."

By the time I had gotten home, there were two messages on Mom's answering machine. One was *GMA* with an actual date for my appearance, the other was a message to call yet another segment producer from *Letterman.*

Mom called *GMA* first. She spoke to the producer of the segment, then I spoke to the producer. They gave me what's called a pre-interview for a half hour on the phone. I was to appear Wednesday morning at 8:40 A.M. They'd send a car for us at 6:30 A.M. That meant I had to get up at 4:30 A.M. so I could be in our home studio warming up by 5:00 A.M. I had to have an hour and a half of practice under my belt in the morning before I had to leave. That's what made me comfortable, so that's what I'd have to do. Five O'clock in the morning is very early for a violinist to be playing.

The Letterman interviews went on by phone for the rest of the day. I must have spoken to five different people from the show. They kept trying to get us to appear on their show first. But my mom had given her word to *GMA*, and she did not go back on her word— at least not as long as I've known her! The producers from *Letterman* explained it's all about "the get," and they'd "get" me at some later time.

That was disappointing, but I had *GMA* to look forward to. I couldn't wait. It was in two days.

CHAPTER 8

GMA

It was Tuesday. One day before *Good Morning America,* and I was supposed to go to school and act as though nothing had happened. Right! School was its usual cast of technicolor characters. As I took out my books from my locker, just before first period, I saw Tamara Diamond glide down the hall with her entourage (never travel without one). Tamara was the epitome of the popular middle-school girl. She stopped in front of her locker, and I watched for a moment as she engaged in hair flipping, gum snapping, and meaningful shoe comparisons with the other members of her clique. Watching the entourage was like peering at an amusingly choreographed Broadway show. All of them cooing and gesturing in turn, comparing their AOL screen names: Tamz 1, Cutsey—u, Bettyboop—it only gets worse.

I heard the first bell. I ran into class, books open and ready to copy notes. You can spend an entire period in middle school just copying notes, so you really better be able to handle yourself with a ball point pen!

Just as class was starting, Bobby Piccolo rose from his seat, shoulders curved inward, head downcast, and inched his way toward the teacher's desk.

"Uh, excuse me, Mrs. Maplethorpe. I know you won't believe this but I had my homework just this morning, and on the way to school I got accosted by a pack of wild schnauzers. I mean they were totally out of control—barking, scratching and leaping. They wouldn't leave till they usurped the contents of my backpack. I'm lucky I'm still alive."

Bobby took a dramatic pause, looking at Mrs. Maplethorpe out of the corner of his eye to check the effect of his monologue. Mrs. Maplethorpe was not amused. Her lip began to twitch (twitching is not good . . . when they start with the twitching, bad things follow), and her brow began to levitate. Her nostrils flared, and one wondered if the smoke would be far behind.

"That's it! I've had it! Everyday, Bobby, you have another sad-sack tale about why you don't have your homework. If you can't manage to produce the homework needed for this class, I suggest you leave. Go down to Mr. Palmetto's office immediately. Let's see if we can put you out of your misery."

It was getting a little ridiculous already. It was three quarters of the way through the first semester, and Bobby must have made up 200 stories about why he never had his work: wild schnauzers, vicious chihuahua, pink elephants, and who knows what else. I felt kinda' sorry for Bobby because, all in all, he wasn't a bad kid, he just couldn't get himself together.

Well, those were the most interesting of the morning's events. My mom came to pick me up at 11:36 again and more news came with her.

"Joey you got two more amazing calls today. First of all, the producers of the *Caroline Rhea Show* called (she took over for Rosie O'Donnell when her show went off the air), and they want you to appear for a guest performance and interview. That will be next Tuesday. Then a reporter from the *New York Times* called. Joey, they are going to do a full-page article on you. They've been following your story over the past couple of articles, they visited your web site, and called the conductor you'll be working with at Lincoln Center in October. They are all prepared for an interview with you. They'll be at our house next Monday, the day before the *Caroline Rhea Show.*"

"Whoaaa! I can't believe this is all happening."

"I know. Can you handle all this?"

"Of course, are you kidding?"

"Well Joey, these things tend to feed on themselves. They snowball very quickly, and they can get out of control. It might be too much stress coming at you all at once. I'm getting a little concerned," Mom remarked.

"Look Mom, you snooze you lose, right?" I said.

"That's true," she admitted. "Let's have a pact. If at any time you feel like everything is too overwhelming, with school and American Institute of Music and concerts and interviews and TV appearances . . ."

"And conductors," I added gleefully.

"Ah yes, and conductors . . . you'll tell me and we'll cut stuff out, all right?"

"Sure. Can any of that stuff we cut out be studying for tests?"

"No, I don't think tests are negotiable here," said Mom good naturedly.

"It's a deal," I said.

"For now let's take one thing at a time. Tomorrow

is *Good Morning America,* so tonight you'll get your homework done, read a little and go to bed early. I'll wake you at 4:30 A.M."

"It'll be an adventure," I said.

"Oy," my mom said.

The next morning, Mom came into my room at 4:30 A.M. It was so dark out, you couldn't see the difference between the shades being drawn or open. I didn't care. This was going to be one of my greatest adventures. National TV—Diane Sawyer. I was so psyched.

By 5:00 A.M. we were in the studio. My mom ran practices like an efficient Swiss time piece. You could time a soufflé by our practice. I ran my scales and arpeggios, thirds, sixths, tenths and octaves. I was ready to perform the pieces. Even though I was going to play three minutes and thirty seconds of Sarasate's *Introduction and Tarantella,* I had to play a couple of other pieces first in practice to warm up my fingers thoroughly. The *Tarantella* was a devilishly fast and technically nerve-wracking piece. I had to be thoroughly ready for it. Also like clockwork, at 6:15 A.M., before the limousine showed up, Ms. Liebling called to hear my piece over the phone. How's that for dedication? In this business, if you don't have both your entire family and your teacher devoted to you, you don't have a prayer of making it.

The set for *Good Morning America* was awesome. It was a downtown subway station set filled with lights and color. There was a small stage covered in red carpeting, with a Steinway grand piano on it. All the way around us were floor to ceiling windows, filled with the passersby of New York. They peered through the glass and waved periodically

The sound technicians had me do the opening of my piece ten times before my actual camera time came. They had to make sure the balance was right. It wasn't often they got to mic a violin for a classical performance. *Good Morning America* didn't have too many of those on their news shows. I didn't mind in the least. I had a ready made and appreciative audi- ence—the stage crew and the people pulled in from off the streets that make up their small group of on-cam- era onlookers. I'd play for about one minute, everyone would applaud, they'd do further sound checks and the whole procedure would begin again. It's such a big job to get a performance to work perfectly over the air.

The main techi was named Jett. He was a very cool guy—he sported a braid down his back, a bicycle mustache which pointed up at the ends, and several tattoos on the top of his arms. He didn't look like he'd be working on *GMA*, but he certainly knew his stuff. He made my little violin sing through the airwaves. I was so impressed. He slipped me his business card and said he'd be happy to "do the sound" on my first CD—when I was ready. Imagine that!

Finally the sound engineer gave me the final countdown to my segment. Onto the stage walked Diane Sawyer—this was for real. Three, Two, One:

"Today we have the great pleasure of welcoming a true prodigy, Josef Cohen . . ."

Oh wow, now she was talking about me. Before I knew it, she had announced the name of the piece I was playing that morning. I nodded to Luba and off we went. As I played the last chord I could feel in my bones that it was the best I had ever performed the

Tarantella. The studio audience erupted in applause, the sound engineers gave me the thumbs up, the other crew members hooted hurrahs and Diane Sawyer invited me back for the following season. It was a moment! I didn't want to leave.

CHAPTER 9

THERE ARE NO MIRACLES

I didn't see Zayde that week until the family Chanukah dinner on Thursday. It was at our house this year because Zayde was so sick. The next day we'd be heading to Florida. My family hadn't taken a vacation since last year. We were ready for one. I wasn't really prepared for the way Zayde looked. The bell rang and I ran to the door.

"Grandma, Zayde." I flung my arms around them like a blanket. Then I took a good look at Zayde. He looked like a very old man. Older than I'd ever seen him. Scary old—and terribly thin. I bit my lip and didn't say a word.

"Come on in, guys, we're all ready to start," I said. Mom took Grandma's coat and hung it on the middle hangar next to my black winter coat. That way its light color would stand out from the other coats in the closet when she went to get it. Grandma had cataracts and it was hard for her to determine colors right now. She needed a cataract operation, but who could think about more operations with Zayde so sick. I took Zayde's coat and draped it over our living room chair so he wouldn't have to go hunting for it later. I led them both over to the table.

My mother lit the Channukah candles and we all

sang the *brachas*. Everything looked festive—the beautiful table, the multi-colored candles in their highly-polished silver holders, the special china—but a heavy sadness hung in the air.

After dinner, Zayde explained that he had developed cellulitis in his legs. That's when fluid collects in the legs and they get all swollen and red as if a painter had taken his choicest screaming red and brushed it on from knee to toes. The doctor said Zayde would have to get intravenous antibiotics, so he had to enter the hospital tomorrow.

Now they tell us. We were going to be in mid-air, on our way to Florida at the time Zayde was to be admitted. But I guess he wanted it that way. He didn't want us to even think about canceling our trip on his account. Mom was very uneasy about this whole thing, but she never said we should cancel. She spoke to my dad in hushed tones after dinner. I have no idea what was said, but we wound up going to Florida the next morning and Zayde wound up going to the hospital as planned. I knew it was the last Channukah.

Each day in Florida we called the hospital to talk to Zayde. On and off he sounded pretty good. He was bored, but his legs were getting less swollen he said, so that was a plus. He couldn't wait to get home.

"I can think of more exciting things to do than sitting here watching my legs deflate," he laughed. "I'd much rather be hearing you play."

"Soon," I said, "soon."

"So what are ya doin' over there? The weather sure must be better than here. I'm looking out the window everyday and seeing nothing but rain."

"Well, I'm playing golf; at least I'm learning how to

. . . the instructor says I have a good swing."

"Well, don't hit anyone in the head. That's the first rule." He laughed at his own joke.

"Okay, Zaydl. I won't. My tennis is good, and I'm swimming a lot. I even get to do a shorter practice while I'm down here—only two hours. It's a pleasure."

"You sound great, Joey. Have a wonderful time. You're a good boy. By the time you're back home, I'll be back home."

For the rest of the vacation, I tried not to think about Zayde. It sounds cruel, I know, but that's how I get through things. My mom always says we each do what we have to, to get through. This is what I have to do.

When we returned home, we all went to visit Zayde. As we walked into the house, Grandma took my mom aside and did some more whispering. The problem with that is that Grandma has hearing trouble, so when she whispers, she automatically speaks at almost a normal pitch. Needless to say, I heard everything. Zayde came home from the hospital unable to walk at all. He went in able to walk slowly with a walker; he came home totally weak and unable to move. They did more CAT scans in the hospital. It seems as though the cancer had spread to his spine, lungs, stomach, and liver—everywhere. The doctor said three months now. How do you go from six months to three months in less than three weeks? Mom looked like she was in shock. Grandma held it together.

I walked into Zayde's room to see him. Zayde looked like death. Three months, I thought? How about three weeks. Who are they kidding? There's nothing left of him? Is this what happens when you put your faith in doctors?

Grandma had said that Zayde's doctor didn't come to see him once while he was in. Mom said that was because he had written Zayde off already. So much for bedside manner. At what point, I wondered, does a doctor decide you're no longer worth the effort? One month, two months left? Do some give up at six months? This was amazing to me. We were talking about my grandfather's life here. The life of Gershon Levinson. A human being par excellence. A great man. Doesn't that doctor know that Zayde is a great man? Don't they offer classes in humanity in medical school?

"Hi Zaydl," I said quietly. He was resting.

"Hey Joey," he replied weakly.

"I was waiting for you. Come in. Come sit." His speech was very slurred now. He was skin and bones. I mean his round colorful cheeks were hollow—sunken. I just saw him ten days before, he didn't look like this. How can that happen so quickly? I sat down on the chair next to his hospital bed. He had a hospital bed now and a commode. He couldn't move anymore. Only his arms. They stretched out to me.

I have to admit I was a little afraid to hold his hands. I know that sounds ridiculous. Cancer isn't catching. But it's so scary. I mean you see a person totally whittled away.

"So I leave you for ten days and this is what happens?" I tried to make a joke out of it all.

"Yeah Joey, it's a pretty bad state of affairs, huh?"

"Grandma is trying to get a nurse's aid or companion to help in the house on a daily basis, now. You should have been here for the scene yesterday. Grandma called a Russian & Polish agency and they said they were sending down two possible candidates. The call went something like this . . ."

This was Zayde at his prime—retelling a great story, complete with accents and idiosyncrasies. He always loved to do that, and obviously still did.

" 'Vell,' the owner of the agency said, 'I chave two ladies. Vun's named Manna and the other is Nana. Vun is older, the other is younger; vun is smarter, the other, vell, not so smart, but she drives and the other doesn't. Vun is strong like ox, the other is small like bird—but she reads English. You set up couch in den vith hospital bed so dey can sleep in same room vith your chusband, okay?'

Zayde had a big smile on his face now. I couldn't keep from smiling, too.

"So Grandma said, 'What do I need both of them to stay over night for?'

" 'Not both of dem; you choose—only vun stays— you choose vich vun.'

" 'Ah, okay,' nodded Grandma 'how will I know who has more English?'

"I told her to ask them a lot of questions, and whoever keeps saying, 'okay, okay' to everything she said, that's the one who has no idea what she's talking about.

"Then Grandma asked what I thought was actually the six million dollar question, 'What if the one who drove the two of them here was the one we picked to stay? How does the other one get home? She'll have no English, no money, and then, no car. Am I supposed to pay for a taxi all the way home for them?'

"Well, they don't live in Poland," I told her. He was on a roll now. Then I told Grandma to make sure to have them each read the medication labels. Anyone who read them like 'methakakabakanol,' was not the girl for me!" He chuckled a little and coughed.

Even though his speech was very low and severely slurred, I still understood every word. I sat close and listened to my zayde's great sense of humor.

"So is there more Zaydl?" I asked.

"Of course. There's always more," he added with a sarcastic sigh.

"The two of them came, Grandma picked one. . . . I think it was Nana, but who can know for sure? . . . The other one, luckily, was the one who drove, so she left. Then we had some fun. Nana could speak only a little English, but she had a loud voice and Grandma speaks no Polish or Russian, and she's hard of hearing. So the two of them spent the day pantomiming and yelling, back and forth. No one was getting mad, because the yelling wasn't a mad yelling, it was so Grandma could hear what Nana was saying. I tell you, I hadn't heard that much excitement since I landed at New Guinea in WWII."

I thought the end of the story was as funny as the beginning. Zayde continued, "Grandma told Nana that it wasn't working out, so Grandma would pay her the full amount and she should pack up and leave in the morning. Nana wouldn't go. She said, 'Oh please Mrs., the agent berry, berry bad woman. She take my passport, she no give it back if I don't keep job. I must stay and get paid for full week. Please Mrs., no send me home,' " Zayde finished with a big sigh.

"Grandma must have been so upset, what did she

94

do? She didn't sign anything to pay her for days she wasn't working, right? She was just trying the woman out," I said, concerned.

"You don't mess with Grandma," Zayde said. "She wasn't gonna' be taken by anyone. She said 'if you don't pack your bags I'll pack 'em for you. I have a sick husband here and he needs the proper care and you can't give it. What is this, the Russian/Polish Mafia? I'm paying you and asking you to leave. I'll call the police if you don't.'

"At that, Nana/Manna whoever she was, got very excited and started running around the room with her hands up in the air screaming: 'polizia, polizia, oh no Mrs. . . . I go, I go.' To make a long story short, Nana/Manna left. Grandma called a cab to take her to a train that would take her to another train that would connect with another train that would get her close enough to her apartment in Brooklyn. Grandma proceeded to call another agency and hope for the best."

I couldn't believe this story. I guess it was hard to find the right care giver for someone who was dying. Zayde wanted to stay at home. That was his wish, and that was ours too.

Over the next two days different companions and aides came to the house. They finally had to hire three in total. You see, hospice only gives you four hours a day of care, five days a week—that was from 9:00 A.M.—1:00 P.M. (That's really cheap. What kind of help is that for a dying man?) So then you have to find someone to stay from 1:00 P.M.—7:00 P.M., and then someone else to stay through the night, not to mention weekends. Grandma could no longer take care of

Zayde. It was just too much. So, they had Peggy from hospice in the morning, Danni in the afternoon, and Stephanie at night.

When I returned that week, I brought my violin to play for Zayde. I wanted him to hear my new concert repertoire. I walked into the den and Zayde was on an oxygen machine. It seems as though he had had an episode in the morning where he couldn't catch his breath. They thought this was it! But the nurse ordered in some oxygen immediately and that stabilized him. Zayde looked up at me weakly and smiled. He didn't say anything. Grandma explained that he had stopped eating two days before and hadn't started again. He wasn't speaking much either—just breathing. It seemed like he was concentrating on just breathing. He sure knew it was me though. His eyes still twinkled and he motioned me with his hand to play. I took out my violin and gave a command performance of *Zigeunerweisen.* He loved it. I could tell. It was the last time I would ever play for my grandfather.

Well, you know the rest. That weekend was the last we ever spent together. Now, here I was on a train bound for Manhattan, soon to disembark and meet a legend. So much had happened in my life to bring me to this point—but nothing prepared me for life with Mischa.

CHAPTER 10

LOOKING FOR UNCLE MISCHA

Uncle Mischa was supposed to meet me when I disembarked at Grand Central Station. He never showed up. This was my first inkling of how things were to be. I guess I wasn't too surprised after all the stories I had heard. But I did know that if I ever got to practice with him during the weeks of my stay, I'd become a greater technician and a more sensitive musician. So, which was more important anyway—responsibility or musicality? I chose musicality. I could deal with the rest.

So, I flagged down a yellow taxi and gave him the address, "1325 West 66th Street, please." Off we went. I had this very unsettled feeling. I should have felt as if I were going home, but I didn't; I just hoped that the time would come, at some point in my future, where Manhattan would feel like home.

The building was rather contemporary and very tall. More bland looking on the outside than I had expected from my uncle, but one never knows what lies within.

I took the elevator to the 7th floor and walked to the right, toward apartment 7K. I would have rung the doorbell but since the door was slightly ajar, I placed my hand tentatively on the knob and walked in.

"Hello? Any one here?" I called. I heard some rustling in the living room which was just off the foyer. I was so busy trying to be brave that I forgot to notice anything at all about the apartment. That was unusual for me. I walked toward the rustling.

"Hello. I'm Joey, Mischa Golub's nephew."

"Ah, if it isn't the wee one from Connecticut. Aren't you cute as a button?"

I didn't know, was I supposed to answer that?

"I'm Mathilde, Mr. Golub's housekeeper—actually I like to think of meself as his assistant, 'cause God only knows what would happen around here to yer uncle if I weren't there to organize his life. My friends call me Matti, you can too. In fact, even yer uncle sometimes calls me Matti, when he's not in a huff, which he usually is, but I don't suppose you know that about him either, eh?"

There was another one. Was I supposed to answer that too? It didn't matter, because sooner than I could ever answer, Matti started talking again.

He fergot to pick ya up I suppose. Well that's Mr. Golub for ya. He means well, but he gets so involved . . . don't ask me with what now, because I swear to God I don't know. He disappears inside that room there," she pointed to the right. "That's his studio . . . well, at least the man calls it his studio, who knows what it is or what goes on in there. All I ever hear in there is shattering glass and paper rustling. I call and call but does he answer? No sir, he doesn't. What can ya do with such a man? As long as he comes outa' there in one piece I figure he's ahead of the game. And he stays in there, I tell ya, days on end. You'd think he was in there with the wee people fixin' to do some

98

nasty prank, you would. I've worked for yer uncle fer fifteen years, and he still never lets me set eyes on that room.

Suddenly we heard, Smaaasssh! Crackle, crackle, slam! The sound of glass breaking and books banging and who knows what else!

"Is he all right in there?" I asked, concerned.

"Ya see what I'm talkin' about lad? He's as loony as a woodpecker without a beak, he is! But, it's good, steady work, and he stays out of me way—most of the time."

"Mathilde, can I ask you a question?"

"Fire away, young one?"

"Was he always alone like this? I mean, didn't he ever have a girlfriend or a bunch of buddies?"

Now Mathilde was quiet . . . for the first time since I opened the door, she had nothing to say.

"Ah, I should just keep me big mouth shut. I swear, sometimes I go on and on and . . ."

"Mathilde, stop. It's okay, really, if you don't want to tell me. I was just curious. That's one part of his life my grandma never talked about."

I knew there was a story there somewhere because Matti had been cleaning the same spot on the desk for the past five minutes.

"Ah well, seeing as how yer uncle may not allow us to enjoy his company fer days now, I might as well tell ya a story. Sit, lad." I sat down on the overstuffed Chintz couch that engulfed my uncle's living room. A talkative Irish maid employed by my eccentric Russian, American, Jewish uncle was now going to tell me a secret about his life that I had yet to hear from my grandparents. This was going to be worth the trip, I could tell.

"Did ya ever hear, young Joe, that yer uncle was once married?"

"What? Married?" I choked on my saliva as I gasped. Not that it was a bad thing to discover that Mischa had been married, it was just such a surprise. "To whom? When? What happened to her?" I was sure Matti would tell me some ghoulish tale of how the girl followed my uncle into his study and never came out. The shattering of glass was the last thing heard.

"Okay. One thing at a time, Joe. When yer uncle Mischa had already established himself as an important violin teacher, he began being invited to lots of opening night concerts at different big halls all over the country. One night, twenty years ago, he walked into The Boston Pops Symphony Hall and heard what he thought was a nightingale on the stage. There, before him, was an angelic looking young soprano, a songbird, Joey, with a lyric coloratura voice, just like the Irish girls have, ya know . . . but I digress! Anyway, she wore a pink lace gown with little pink and white flowers at the shoulders. Her hair was blonde and long with curls, and yer uncle says, her eyes were the color of the morning sky on a crisp New England day. Her name was Marta Halend, and yer uncle fell hard fer her, he did."

I was speechless. I didn't say a word because I didn't want Matti to stop speaking. I was afraid she'd leave out some vital detail. Boy, if I were a writer like that kid Greg I'd be taking all this down at break neck speed.

"Well, after the concert, yer uncle met some of the musicians from the orchestra and went back stage.

Lots of people knew Mr. Golub, so he must have seemed like a celebrity to young Marta. When she saw him for the first time he was surrounded by violinists. The conductor took her hand and brought her over to yer uncle.

"Allow me to introduce you to Ms. Marta Halend," the conductor said to Mr. Golub.

"She is going to be the next big thing, Mischa," added the maestro.

Oh boy, there was that statement again. You'd think media and people in the business would be so tired of hearing that already. It makes an artist sound like sliced cheese.

"Evidently yer uncle kissed her hand, complimented her performance and, somehow, though God knows how, because he is surely not suave, asked her out. This was the beginning of a whirlwind romance. The two of them were seen everywhere together. Yer uncle changed his teaching schedule constantly to fly to Boston to be with Marta, and she would concertize in the New York metropolitan area as much as possible. They went to opening nights on Broadway, opera, orchestral performances, gallery openings—anything and anywhere in the arts scene, they were there. Yer uncle was truly smitten.

Eventually, they couldn't bear to be parted, so Mr. Golub popped the question. Marta joyfully responded yes and the date was set. It was June 28th—a Saturday. The wedding was to take place on the Great Lawn in Tanglewood. The whole arts community was buzzing about the event.

Then came a terrible blow. The night before the wedding, Marta came to yer uncle's house. She was in tears. She said she had wanted to tell him for months but couldn't summon up the courage. It appears that Marta had a severe heart condition. It was genetic. Her doctors never wanted her to sing because of the further strain it put on her heart, but Marta said she was born to sing, and had to take her chances. A life without music was not worth living. Well, lad, now it was too late. Evidently her heart had become very weak. The doctors couldn't tell her when it would give out, only that it would, shortly."

I couldn't believe my ears. It was a major motion picture I was hearing, not a moment in the life of someone in my family. It was the thing Academy Awards are made of.

"Well, me lad, yer uncle didn't know where to turn, what to do. This was the love of his life—a life that had so many disappointments. Marta begged him to go through with the wedding. Yer uncle was so torn. He loved her so much, but didn't feel he could face the unbearable heart-ache of losing his wife at any moment. He decided to go through the motions of it, and then, do what his gut told him."

"So what did his gut tell him?" I couldn't hold back anymore. I had to know what happened.

"So, the day of the wedding came. The sun rose and shone on the open field where all that beautiful music is made everyday all summer. The white tent was put up, an orchestra played, Marta, so beautiful, walked down a white satin aisle to meet her love. Yer uncle stood, trembling at the front of all the pews. They exchanged vows. They cried. They kissed, at least that's how I heard it. Then, they walked each other out of the tent and down the lawn to the field where the party had been set.

Everyone was busy greeting guests when the band signaled the first dance—the dance of the bride and the groom. Marta swept up the aisle, radiant and hopeful, but there was no sign of her groom. The band played the intro several times—but still no sign of yer uncle."

"So where was he? Did he pass out? Did he leave the party?" I prodded.

"Oh yeah, He left the party all right. He left the state. Yer uncle drove home in a cold sweat, changed clothes and got on the first train for Manhattan. By the next day he had had the marriage annulled. That was the last time he saw his Marta, and the last time he set foot in a concert hall. That's how the tale goes, young Joe. That's the long and the short of it."

"You mean he hasn't been out in the arts community or to a concert since he was thirty?"

"No, of course not. He was mortified. Humiliated. Heart broken."

"Is there any more I should know?" I was almost afraid to ask.

"Well, since you asked, Marta lived for six more months. Those who never knew about her heart condition thought she died of a broken heart. They didn't know how right they were."

"Wow. Do you think Uncle Mischa is a bad man for doing this?"

"Me? Who am I to judge anybody? He's not a bad sort. He's a tormented sort. It's his life to be tormented. Those are the cards he was dealt. Can't ya see?"

"I guess she should have been honest with him at first, right? It's not his fault if he couldn't handle it."

"I may question his timin' but not his motive. He never meant to hurt her. But he knew what he could handle, that's all. A man's gotta know himself."

At that moment, Uncle Mischa emerged from his studio. At least I assumed it was my uncle. He certainly looked the part: long salt and peppered hair down to his shoulders, sort of wild looking, as if the teeth of a comb had never had the pleasure of meeting his scalp. His eyes were sharp and almost black in color. His face had a 5:00 shadow, but it was only 10:00 A.M., and he wore all black—a black silk shirt, baggy black trousers and a long black morning coat trailing behind him. He was a vision out of a gothic drama.

"Well now, it's about time, Master Golub. What are ya doin' in there when yer nephew comes to visit for the first time? Are ya daffy, man?"

I couldn't believe Matti could speak so casually to my uncle. Wasn't she afraid of him? I must have had a look of dread on my face because she continued . . .

"Ah, he's a pussy cat, yer uncle, just a wee bit unuuuuusual."I loved the way she spoke. You could tell she was born and raised in Ireland. It was the most delicious sound. It was like music. No wonder my uncle put up with her.

"Where is my Tchaikovsky score," Mischa grumbled, "What did you do with it now, woman?"

"I wouldn't be takin' yer score now, would I Mr. G? You musta' lost it somewhere in that hell hole of a studio you have there. I'll be happy to look for it there, you know." The corners of her lips turned upward in a mischievous smile. She would have loved to get into that studio.

"Ach, 15 years and she's still trying to get into my inner sanctum," scoffed Uncle. "I put it here on the coffee table."

"Well surely ya didn't, 'cause it would be there."

"Well, I know where I put my music, woman."

"Aye, and this score got so fed up with ya that it grew wings and flew outa' this apartment, did it?"

"No, but you rearranged my coffee table."

"Look man, nothin's been rearranged in this room but yer head. Look for it on the piano."

Mischa went reluctantly over to the Steinway. There, right on the top, was the Tchaikovsky score.

"Aha!" He exclaimed. I knew you moved it."

"Aha? Aha what? Impossible man!" Matti huffed under her breath.

It wasn't until this moment that Mischa turned and acknowledged me.

"So you're my sister's boy? I hear you're good."

"Thank you," I replied, "I hear you're extraordinary."

"Ha!" He twinkled, "You shouldn't believe everything you hear. Where are your bags?"

"This bag and my violin are all I have. I'm not sure where to put them, though."

"Come with me. I'll show you to your room. Matti, what's the matter with you? You too busy wagging your tongue to show my nephew his room?"

"Aye, and you're too busy talkin' to leprechauns in there" (she pointed to his studio), to get to the station to meet him! Exasperatin' man"

They looked at each other and laughed out loud. I didn't know if I could get used to this kind of daily banter. I couldn't tell if they were playing or angry with each other. What a difference from life with my parents. I always knew where I stood with them. Now I was in the middle of a rapid fire competition of wits.

Mischa led me to the door next to his studio. I pushed it open and saw a most curious sight. It was a large room with peach colored walls and record album covers from floor to ceiling, except in the middle of the room. There, before me, dangling from the ceiling was a chandelier made exclusively of old, yellowed orchestral scores. My uncle chuckled when he saw the expression on my face:

"When I need more light I just put a match to the chandelier!" He laughed. "It also works as a space heater! HAHA!"

Uncle Mischa was getting such a kick out of himself. He must not have had much company around the apartment, except for his students.

"Put your things by the bed, come have something to eat, and then you can get practicing."

Well, that sure was fast. Food then music. I wondered how long he was going to make me practice each day. I was afraid to ask. So I didn't.

"Great," I replied, and plopped my bag and violin case on the right side of the bed. There was no phone or TV in my room, so I didn't guess he expected me to do much of anything except study and practice, and read by "fire-light!"

Matti fixed me a nice brunch of scrambled eggs and cheese (one of my favorites), an English muffin and orange juice. The smells evoked these wonderful memories of Grandma and Zayde's house. I was suddenly terribly homesick. I took a few deep breaths and got my violin. I set up my collapsible stand in my new room, tuned the fiddle and got to work: open strings, scales, arpeggios. I took my time to make sure my arm was flowing—legato. It sounded pretty good to me. I knew my uncle would be listening to every note. This was kind of like an audition. I began my pieces. There was quiet for about ten minutes into my short concert repertoire, then I heard from directly outside my door:

"Oy, terrible. Oh, please stop, you're killing the mice in my apartment! That's the worst sound I ever heard a viola make."

"Uncle," I called, "that's my violin."

"Oy, even worse," he said. "Why don't you leave out the bottom part of the chords and just play the top?"

"But that's not how it's written. It's disrespectful to the composer." I opened my door.

"Believe me, the composer is listening right now and dying his second perfect death," and he put his hands on his neck and pretended to choke—"eeeee-hch!"

We broke out hysterically laughing. This would become the routine for our practices. I would start and not ask for his help. He'd wait till he heard things that were intolerable to him, then he'd let me have it with his biting, sarcastic sense of humor. I was expected to take it well (just like Matti), and then he'd come and practice with me, making each line infinitely more beautiful than I could have without him. He was a master, no question about it.

Every so often, within the three hours that we worked together daily, Matti would really like the piece we were doing so she'd start humming along in the background. This would get Mischa's back up!

"Confound it, woman, can't you hear the boy has

enough trouble with the written music? He doesn't need to hear your rendition as well!"

"Hummmpph!" Matti would sniff.

Before I knew it, I was settling into life as a Manhattanite—and life with Mischa. He turned out to be a terrific uncle, although somewhat eccentric. He practiced with me, made me laugh, teased and inspired me into playing on a higher level. He expected a great deal of me, but I figured I was up to the challenge. Best of all, Ms. Liebling was thrilled with my progress. She would say things like: "Ah my schatsy, that was such a wonderfully organized performance; so many good things, schatsy. I'm so proud of you." School was . . . well, school—I'd rather keep my expectations low and be pleasantly surprised.

When I would get a little hot under the collar from too much work, Mischa would take me for a spin in his 1955 Chevrolet. It was a gas-guzzling jalopy—not a thing of beauty but it ran, and served as a good diversion. People in the city are so funny about their cars. The happiest days of their lives are when they get a new car, and when they sell their new car. Mischa never took his car anywhere, he just drove it around town. He never parked it anywhere either. He just pulled it right back into the lot. He said having someplace to go meant you had to have a definite time to get there and a definite time to return home. And, with city traffic, that was just too much pressure for him!

This same strange psychology is evident, I think, in the reason that many people buy apartments in the city. They've spent their life's savings to buy a place in Manhattan, just so they can make enough money there to move out of Manhattan. Of course my uncle was the exception. He was never going to leave Manhattan. It was in his blood. He said that it's the only city in the world where you can walk in the streets and smell music.

By the next week I felt like quite the independent New Yorker. On Saturday, I arrived a few minutes early to A.I.M. Professor Krantz had asked me to pick up the Ur-text for the *Bach Sonata and Partitas* before my morning orchestra rehearsal. A.I.M.'s bookstore was bound to have it; it has everything. I glanced through the Bach files and found a Henle edition and a Behrenreiter. One edition had fingerings marked, one didn't. It would be better to have the fingerings for a first reading I thought, but what if my teacher wanted to put in his own, and I had already learned these fingerings. That would be a pain.

While I was pondering my future purchase, Valery strode into the store, flanked by two gorgeous girls who, I assumed, were pianists (since they weren't carrying their instruments—that's always a dead give away!). He threw back his head in laughter as he entered, and his long dip of bangs followed suit—his eyes gleaming with conquest. The girls hung on his every word.

"Ve chave to find these young ladies some Beethoven Sonatas. Shirley darling, can you chelp us locate them?"

Shirley was the manager of the bookstore, a woman about 60 years old, and totally amused but not taken in by Valery.

"Valery, everything is alphabetized against the wall. I'm sure you can handle it. Just look under "B" for Mr. Beethoven," she smiled.

"Shirley, you chave such a delightful sense of chumor!" Valery winked and led his "women" over to the "B" section, which is where I was still pondering my Bach selection.

"Hi Valery!"

"Chey, leettle fiddler. Girls, do you know this great, young violinist, Josef Cohen? He chas big, fiery spirit. Packs a . . . chow you say . . . wollop on that fiddle. Josef, this is Lara and Petunia."

Petunia?

"Nice to meet you," I blushed and answered, but not necessarily in that order.

"Oh, he's so cute!" cooed Lara.

"Sweet!" Petunia chimed in.

"Oh come on. I'm getting jealous," Valery teased.

It dawned on me that he was the one I had to speak to about Catherine. He would know just how to get her to go out with me. Now that I was a "man about town," I felt I could turn my attention to my most pressing social concern—Cat.

"Uh, Valery, could I speak to you about something . . . privately?"

"Of course, leettle fiddler. Excuse me ladies, my public calls."

We walked over to the corner by the sweatshirts.

"I need some advice from the pro. You see, there's a girl . . ."

"Say no more. You burn for cher, you bleed for cher, you must make cher yours!"

"Well, actually, I just wanted to ask cher, I mean, her out."

Valery put his hand on my shoulder and began

with a theatrical swoop of his head.

"Ah, you must think big, you must think romantic, you must think . . . middle school musical! Then, perchaps, Starbucks. Nothing says, 'I care' like a Mocha Venti."

"You think?"

"Why not? She lives nearby. Maybe you can ask her on a Saturday when she can use a night out after conservatory?"

"It sounds like a plan to me. Actually, the show is this weekend, and I hadn't planned on going because I really don't know the kids that well yet; but I'll give it a shot! Thanks Valery."

"Anything to chelp in issues of the cheart, leettle fiddler."

Valery walked off with a confident gait and joined forces with his sidekicks.

"Goodbye, Shirley darling." He left the store. What a guy!

I had to wait till 4:00 P.M. to ask Cat because that was the end of her last class. I don't think I heard a note of music I played all that day. At 4:00, I ran up to room 506 to meet her at class. I rehearsed my lines as was becoming my tradition.

"Hey, I forgot to ask if you wanted to check out my school show this weekend." Was that too stilted? Yeah, gotta be looser.

"Hey Cat, how was class? What's up for the weekend? Feel like seeing the show at my middle school? I'm going tonight."

That's good. Sounds looser, more nonchalant. The door opened.

"Hey Joey, what ya' doing up here?"

Uh oh. I didn't expect that one.

"Uh, I had to . . . see Dr. Lydian for a second about the homework assignment."

Ooh, that was not convincing. No, no, not good at all. She'll see right through me.

"Oh, cool, I get to have company going down now."

Hmmm, that was nice. I'm company!

"So what's up with you for the weekend?" We jostled our way through the halls of exhausted string players.

"I don't know. Tons of work. Maybe a movie, but nothing planned. You?"

I'm goin' to my middle school musical tonight. It's *Les Miserables*. I thought it would be a fun way to get the feel of my new school—you know, catch the vibe. You wanna' come? We could go to Starbucks afterwards?" *How was I doing, Valery?*

"Wow, that sounds like fun. What time is it?"

"7:00 P.M., and there's a Starbucks right at the corner."

"Come with me so I can ask my mom, Okay?"

"Sure."

We met Catherine's mom by the guard desk and she described the evening's invitation. I could see the corners of her mom's mouth turn up slightly. She knew.

"Fine. Daddy and I will just stay around town tonight and pick you up at the Starbucks at 10:00 P.M."

"Excellent," I said with a huge gust of happiness. Meet ya in my school's lobby at 6:50 P.M."

"See ya later, Joey"

Oh yeah! Oh yeah! Valery is king! I did it, and no

interruption from the troops!

CHAPTER 11

AT THE SHOW

I brushed my teeth for twenty minutes that evening. Twenty minutes, standing in front of a mirror, spitting. I felt ready.

"So, are you meeting anyone at the show, Joey, or you going solo?" asked Uncle Mischa.

"Ah, look at the way he's sparklin'," remarked Matti, "the boy's definitely got a sweetheart!"

"Well, actually, I am meeting Catherine there, I admitted.

"Oh, Catherine? Really. An after hours rendezvous?" teased Mischa. "That's nice." He winked at Matti.

"Yep. I gotta go guys." I bolted.

I reached the middle school at 6:50 P.M. exactly. I always liked to be on time. There was Catherine, standing in the middle of the lobby. She wasn't wearing her violin . . . I almost didn't recognize her!

"Hey, when did ya get here?" I asked.

"Only five minutes ago. I didn't want to miss you."

She didn't want to miss me . . . is that sweet or what? I know I just stood there looking at her for a few moments. I don't think she noticed.

"Let's get our seats." I led her to Row D. She sat down with a heavy sigh.

"Tough day?" I asked playfully. But Catherine didn't look so playful all of a sudden.

"Tough semester. I think I have to drop Chamber Music. My teacher is a maniac. She thinks we can get through an entire trio in four lessons. If I have to learn anymore music, Joey, I'll explode! I was up till 11:00 P.M. on Wednesday, trying to perfect the trio. That's insane. I couldn't study for my math test, and I found out yesterday that I blew the test."

"Wow. I know for you to say this takes a lot. I'm sorry it's such a bad time."

"Yeah. I decided when you asked me to come tonight that I just had to get out and clear my head."

Hmmm, that's the only reason she came?

"I can't even have a normal social life anymore. Violin was never hard for me, you know. I was always able to put in my hours, get my school work done well, and have time to go out. A well-rounded kind of life, you know what I mean?"

No, I didn't really. Lately, it was all about the work. I hadn't really thought about that part much. But now that she mentioned it . . .

"And you know what else? I can tell you 'cause you're my friend . . ."

"What else?" I queried.

"I have this huge crush on Gabriel, and he doesn't give me the time of day."

What? Calm down, deep breath, maybe this isn't as bad as it seems . . . Gabriel? She's always with me, what's she doing thinking about Gabriel?! Breathe, breathe. All color was draining from my face. I could feel it.

"I mean, he doesn't even know I'm alive. I'm always

nice to him. I rush to ear-training class to grab the seat next to him. I bake cookies for him."

Cookies? She never baked cookies for me?

"He's so shy, though. He barely talks to me. But he's so cute, you know with those exotic Spanish good looks. He's always smoldering?"

"Maybe he doesn't like cookies." Okay, it was a stupid response, I admit, but I was totally stunned.

"Oh, come on Joey. You always have good advice. You're so together. What do you do if you like someone and you can't get their interest?"

"Invite them to the middle school show?" I laughed nervously.

"Come on," Catherine whined.

I never heard her whine. This was more serious than I thought. The nerve of her, accepting a date with me 'cause she had to clear her head. I was plenty mad.

"Look, Cat, you can only do so much. If the guy likes you, he'll show it. No matter how shy he is, he should be responding to your overtures, if he likes you."

"So you think he doesn't ?"

"Well, how can he not like you?" I couldn't help myself. Complimenting her came easily to me.

"Oh Joey, you're the best."

Yeah, that's me . . . what a guy . . . if I was the best, she'd be mooning over me instead of Gabriel. What is it with these Russian and Spanish guys? The accent? The culture? The adventure? I come from Southbury —that's exotic. It sure is a different country compared to Manhattan. Maybe I should wear a long cashmere scarf, swing my hair a lot and speak in a tortured tongue. That might change my life!

The house lights began to flicker. It was show time. I felt sick.

I couldn't really tell you how my next week in school was because I was emotionally dead. My heart hurt, and so did my pride. I went to class, came home, did homework, practiced and daydreamed. I couldn't hold it against Catherine if she just wanted to be friends. We were good at that, I guess. I had to let it go. I had to.

Saturday morning came, I got my practice done quickly and zipped right off to pre-college. As I entered the lobby, there was lots of excitement, I walked right into a buzz-saw of gossip.

"Hey Joey, did you hear about Valery? I can't believe it. It's too awful," Catherine shouted.

"What, what? Did he have an accident or something?" I gasped.

"No, no worse . . . worse. He gave up his violin and ran off with a super model."

"WHAT? *Give me a break!* That did *not* happen."

"Oh yes, listen to this."

"I would if I could, but I haven't heard it this loud in here since Pinchas Zuckerman and Itzhak Perlman came in to give a master class together last year. Let's move out of the lobby."

We walked quickly out of the lobby. As we walked, Catherine told me Mr. Machismo's (as I called Valery), tale of woe.

"You can't believe this. Valery was seeing this super model during the past two months, Emmanuelle."

"Emmanuelle what?"

"Just . . . Emanuelle. You know they're all only born with one name!"

"Oh, yeah."

"So, somehow, she talked him into flying back to Paris with her because she plans on starting a film career there. She told him she'll hook him up with her agent. Maybe he could get a walk on."

"A walk-on? Valery doesn't walk, he plays the violin. What's he gonna' do in Paris without the violin?"

"Ah, use the imagination God gave you, Josef."

"Oh yeah, well, besides that. He can't be with her all the time. It's a good deal for her, right? She gets to start a career and has a handsome musician on her arm for all her media events, and he gets to be at her beck and call."

"I know. Can't he see she doesn't love him? She wouldn't ask him to give up everything for her. Music was his life!"

"Yeah, I know, I've heard that before, Catherine. Calm down." (All the girls at A.I.M. were secretly in love with Valery, even if they didn't know what love was yet. Even Catherine.)

"Oh, the injustice of it all!" cried Catherine wringing her hands.

"Well, what did his violin teacher say? What did Maestro Vunderfall say?"

"That's the really scary part. You know how, even Valery, had tremendous respect for Vunderfall? He never questioned him on interpretations or fingerings. Well, it seems that this week, Valery burst into Vunderfall's office."

"He *would* burst . . . why walk when you could burst?"

"Be serious, Josef."

Uh oh, that was two times she called me Josef already, Catherine was definitely hot under the collar.

"So he burst into Vunderfall's office, swung his scarf over his left shoulder, and announced . . . Maestro, I am leaving this burdensome life. I've had quite enough. I'm going to live in Paris with my love."

"And Vunderfall did exactly what when he heard this?" I could hardly contain myself at this point. "He only has one music stand and one metal chair in his office; I doubt he'd want to risk breaking them."

"That was just it, Vunderfall had no reaction. He supposedly paused for a long minute, stared down Valery, fiery eyes to fiery eyes, walked slowly and softly to the door, opened it and pointed his finger."

"Pointed his finger, where? At Valery?"

"No, no . . . into the hall."

"He said nothing?"

"He said nothing."

"He didn't throw anything?"

"He didn't throw."

"Has anyone seen him since?"

"Who? Valery or Vunderfall?"

"Vunderfall."

"Yeah, sure, he's here this morning. He walked in with his little black beret and tweed jacket. He looked the same. But Valery, no one has seen Valery."

"Wow. This is practically an international incident. You think he was just burnt out?"

"Who?"

"VALERY. Stay with me on this Catherine," I laughed. "Valery. Do you think he had been so programmed and burnt out from doing this professionally for so many years that he was looking for an excuse to get out of the business?"

"Hmm . . . it's a theory. I just can't imagine anyone so devoted giving up on their years of training . . . for a girl."

"That's cause you're a girl! From where I'm standing it sounds pretty good!"

"Josef Cohen, you take that back!" Catherine started whacking me with her orchestra music.

"Okay. Okay. Help! Help! Sexual harassment! Haaaaa . . ."

"Oh fine, I'm glad you think this is so funny. The rest of us are devastated."

"Look, Cat, I think it's terrible, too. In fact, I really don't believe it. Valery will be back, you know; I bet ya some time in the next year or two. You don't just throw that talent away. It's not just the years he put in, it's the music that he put out. You can't live for long having a gift like that bottled up inside. It'll make you crazy."

"You really think so. You think he'll come to his senses?"

"Yep, I do. And he'll come back with the same flourish he left with. He'll come walking in, dressed in city chic black from head to toe, a little stubble under his chin—that Parisian look—he'll stand in the middle of the lobby and announce, "I Chave Returned!"

I didn't realize by this point that Mr. Herrington was standing behind us, waiting to use the restroom. He began clapping."

"Cohen," he said, "I always knew you had a flare for the dramatic. If you don't wind up touring the globe, there's a career for you in film writing! Haha!"

His head did a little dance from side to side. He was quite pleased with himself. Besides, he always had a soft spot for me because I was short and so was he. He used to say, "If you're over five feet, get out of my orchestra! Cohen," he'd say, "you're my idol, you can stay!" We'd all have a good laugh.

Catherine and I parted like the Red Sea for Herrington. He went to the restroom, we went to orchestra to wait for him. You can never be too early to orchestra with Mr. Herrington. He loved to see a ready group of musicians sitting in perfect formation, awaiting his downbeat. Ah, the power.

As we entered the practice hall, I saw Chai, the trumpet guy. Chai was not the most jovial of fellows— always had a sour puss on him. I used to think that was from poor mouthpiece position, but I've discovered over the years, it's just from poor attitude. Chai was what you call a "silent killer." You never heard him warm up and you never heard him practicing his orchestra music before Mr. Herrington arrived. He played softer than the other horn players too, so you didn't pay much attention to him. But in each piece we played, Chai had one murderous note. One note so sour . . . so out of tune . . . so disturbing, that Mr. Herrington would have to stop the whole orchestra and find out who hit it.

"Chai????"

"Yes, Mr. Herrington."

"Might that have been . . . youuuuu?"

"Oh, I dunno."

"Lemme' ask ya a question . . . Chaiiiii."

"Yeah."

"Did ya ever notice the resemblance between a

music stand and a spear???? Did ya . . . Chaiiii?"

Mr. Herrington got tremendous pleasure out of pronouncing certain people's names. Chai's was one of them. He used to rev up the saliva in his throat really slowly, so that it was super liquidy, and begin the "Ch" sound. Then he'd just let it rip . . . CCCCH-HHAAAIII. It was astounding, really, for someone who wasn't born in the Middle East.

Catherine and I unpacked our violins and got to our seats just in time for Mr. Herrington to enter the hall. A voice comes whispering out of the middle of the orchestra, "All rise for the grand, high executioner." People started to giggle. The problem with a hall is, even whispers carry pretty well.

"Mr. WUUUUUUUUU? Is that YOUUUUU?" called Mr. Herrington

Mr. Wu was the principal violist in our orchestra. Nobody knew his first name, because for as long as he'd been at The Institute, he had been in Mr. Herrington's orchestra, and Mr. Herrington only called him Mr. Wu. He was a very big, husky Asian kid, 15 years old—about 6'1, 265 lbs., with a furrowed brow—so none of us thought it so smart to approach him and ask him any questions he might take the wrong way—like what his first name was, for example. Therefore, he remained, always—Mr. Wu.

There were many amusing things about Mr. Wu. One, for example was his boots. Every Saturday, without fail, Mr. Wu wore big, black patent-leather boots with rubber soles. Now, this in and of itself would not have been a problem, except for Mr. Wu's penchant for beating time with his right foot. Every time he got into the music, he'd start keeping the rhythm with his foot, pounding on the floor. Mr. Wu had a big foot. Suddenly, while the violins are doing their own intricate patterns of 16th and 32nd notes, we'd hear the metric pounding of the viola's rhythm coming from mid stage (which is where they sat). Mr. Herrington would have to stop the orchestra because the violins were playing their notes with the viola's rhythm. Poor Mr. Herrington. Poor Mr. Wu.

"Mr. WUUUUUUUUU," screamed Mr. Herrington. Are you a drummer or a string player?"

"Uhhh . . ."

"That's right, Mr. Wu, show us how intelligent you are. Do you see these gray hairs, Mr. Wu?" Herrington would point to his own head. "These are not gray hairs." He now started lifting different hairs up on different sections of his head. "These are flutes, these are timpanists, these are violinists, and this one is YOU-UUUU, Mr. WUUUUU."

The orchestra exploded in laughter. No matter what you had to say about Mr. Herrington, you had to love his sense of humor. Well, rehearsal went on, we had fun, and even managed to interpret some Beethoven. Look, sitting in the same chair for two hours reading the same notes over and over could be down right deadly without the right conductor. Mr. Herrington was the right conductor.

The rest of the day went off without a hitch. I had my classes: theory, ear training, scale class, chamber music (I had a great chamber trio— piano, cello and violin), no performance class today so I had no pressure on me. It was a good Saturday. By 3:00 P.M. I was done. I saw my friend Noah in the cafeteria, so I went over for a shmooze.

"Hey, how was your day?"

"Hey Joey, it was okay, but it's still going on. My chamber group was moved to 4:00, so I have to wait here an hour. Ucch, by the time I get home tonight I'll be fried. I was gonna' go to the movies with Lara, but I think I'm just gonna' crash." (Lara was Noah's girl-friend).

"Yeah I know what ya mean. It makes a big differ-ence having that extra hour to hang here. Can you believe other kids are on the field somewhere playing soccer or baseball right about now, then spending the evening at friends' Bar and Bat Mitzvahs?"

Noah laughed, "Tell me about it. I think about it all the time. I'm missin' out on life here. Don't you feel that way?"

"Well, I don't know about that. Missing out on some other peoples' lives maybe, but this is a big part of my life. I'm supposed to do this."

"Supposed to and wanting to are two different things. It's a major bummer. I didn't want any of this. I mean I know I'm good, but you guys are great. If I can't do as well as you in conservatory, how am I sup-posed to make a go of it in the real world? And if I'm never gonna' make it out there, what am I doin' in here?"

"Noah, you're delirious! This is a place of learning. You're supposed to make mistakes here, and have an occasional crummy lesson, and get out the kinks in your pieces in front of your peers. We're all just trying to do the best we have inside us here. And sometimes that doesn't allow us to run around all weekend like . . ."

"Like normal thirteen year olds? How about that,

Joey? We're not normal. Ever think of it that way?"

I didn't like where this conversation was going. Noah definitely had some issues I knew little about. I was focused; focused on the process, focused on the goal, always focused, and I didn't like my sense of worth being called into question—not at AIM. That was the one place I felt safe.

"Noah, I'm normal, I don't know about you. I just have different priorities. Dancing at kids' Bar Mitzvahs when I'm not even friendly with the kids being Bar Mitzvahed is not one of my priorities. If they're close friends, I find a way to go for part of it."

"Well, I'm missing four parties this month. Kids think I'm crazy, they don't even care when I tell them I'm playing for Leonard Slatkin? They don't know who he is! You're doing that too, right? The top five students in the pre-college were asked. Slatkin is coming next week on Thursday."

"I don't know. I never heard about it. How'd ya find out?"

"Oh, go up to Ms. Liebling's room. She only told the students she saw today. Have you seen her yet?"

"Nope, but I'm goin' now. Thanks for the tip. And by the way, Noah, you just said it yourself, if you weren't in the top five, you wouldn't have been asked."

Noah just shrugged and went back to eating.

Wow, Leonard Slatkin, big time. He was considered one of the most important conductors of our time. That sure changed the tide of the conversation; and it sure helped me to stop feeling sorry for myself—momentarily. There was always something new and exciting to achieve around here. I loved that. It fueled me. Noah must have been having a bad day, week, month—who knew? Before I knew it I was up on the 4th floor, knocking on Ms. Liebling's door.

"Ah schatsy, I thought I'd see you up here before the end of the day. Did you hear Maestro Slatkin is coming to town?"

"Yes, I just found out from Noah. Am I doing it too?

"Of course you are. Now, I need you here warmed up and ready to play on Wednesday night at 7:30 P.M. Are you planning on bringing Luba to accompany?"

"Umm . . . well, I wasn't planning on any of this, but I'll call her as soon as I get home and arrange it. I'm sure for Maestro Slatkin she'll cancel any other engagements."

"Okay, sweetheart, then I'll count on you to be here at 7:30. Wear something nice for the maestro, but it doesn't have to be a suit."

"I will. Thanks so much for the opportunity, Ms. Liebling." I gave my teacher a huge hug.

"Of course, schatsy."

Off I went, down the hall to the lobby. I couldn't wait to get home and tell Uncle Mischa.

On my way, I noticed Salvadore, Noah, Catherine, Mr. Wu, and Freddy—our timpanist—walking toward me in a rather big hurry.

"Hey, Joey, can you get down to the cafeteria . . . if you don't have a class now?" Noah asked. "Lavinia is down there crying her eyes out and she won't talk to anyone. You're friendly with her . . . you go."

Catherine and I looked at each other.

"I have my chamber group this period, Joey. I can't be late. But I don't want to be a bad colleague," Catherine added sincerely.

"Look, you go, I'm done for the day. I'll talk to her." *What was I getting myself into?*

"Thanks. Let me know what happens. Slip me a note in ear training, okay?"

"Okay. I'll see ya."

I hurried downstairs and saw Lavinia quietly crying in the back left corner, behind a pile of books on her table.

"Hey, Lavinia. What's the matter? Can I help?"

"Oh you wouldn't understand, Joey Cohen. Your life is so different from mine. You'd never understand."

"Lavinia, what are you talking about? I can't understand if you won't tell me what it is I won't understand." *Did I just say that?*

Lavinia began rummaging through her bag for a tissue. I never saw a girl who carried more "stuff." First she took out a nail file, then tweezers, a hairbrush, wallet, small photo album, a rag and a bottle of alcohol (to clean her violin strings), a collapsible umbrella, a bag of pretzels, and an address book—but no tissues. I walked over to the cashier to get her some. When I returned she seemed more composed, albeit just a tad drippy.

"Thanks, Joey Cohen. I don't know what to do. I need advice, but you can't tell my mom I was talking to you about this, okay? Promise me."

"Well, why? What will she do to you if I tell her?" I asked nervously.

"Just promise me, you hear? Please."

"I promise, Lavinia. You can tell me." I was starting to get worried about her. Now this was a new feeling.

"I auditioned for the Meadowmount Program, to study with Professor Viederhoff, and I wasn't accepted. He said I had a lot of talent but my interpretations weren't mature enough yet. So, he didn't take me."

"Oh, I'm sorry, Lavinia. But let's keep this in perspective—it is just a summer program. It will not break your life. You'll try again next summer, and you'll make it."

"No, that's not the point. My mother got so angry. She said that if I don't make the program next summer, she's going to stop my violin lessons, and make me give up everything."

"No, Lavinia, she doesn't mean that."

"Yes, yes she does. She doesn't threaten. She acts. Um, I've already said too much."

"No, no, no, go on. You really think she'd make you give up nine years of your life? Lavinia, no mother would take away an instrument from her daughter if she was as talented and dedicated as you are. You know how many kids are pushed just to practice an hour a day? You're a dream come true for a parent."

"How do you know, Joey Cohen?" (Whenever Lavinia was the slightest bit miffed at me, she'd call me by my full name.)

"How do you know what my mother has to do to get me to sound this way? You know what it's like to be twelve. Did you always want to practice three hours? And when you did, did you do it with all that detail? I'm not really that easy to work with, you know."

I had to admit I probably wouldn't have put in all the detail work if my mom hadn't sat with me during practice and coached me on the notes from the last lesson with Ms. Liebling.

"Look, I'd still put in my time, but I know I wouldn't have been as exact without Mom or, now, my uncle there. They point out all the problems. We're still young, Lavinia. We're supposed to be impatient. It's not a bad thing. It's just the way it is. We're busy doing all this work—watching the bow, listening for intonation, making sure the fingers are curved correctly in each position, making the right kind of vibrato in every section, making sure all the vibratos match, making the bow speak with lots of colors. We're very busy. Someone has to be listening to point out the pitfalls."

"Well, my mother wants it all now. And I have to give it to her, or else. You know I want music as my life's work. I expect to go pro soon. My mom expects it to happen yesterday. Look, you've played Carnegie Hall, you're playing at Lincoln Center already this Fall, you've been on national TV, and you and Catherine have both won competitions. All I've done is been complimented by my teacher and invited to play for Pinchas Zuckerman. It's my turn, and I can't figure out where to turn? I can't let her take this away from me."

"I didn't know you were invited to play for Pinchas Zuckerman."

"So what?"

"Well, Ms. Liebling never invited me to play for Mr. Zuckerman. So you have done something really special that I never did.

While I was saying this I felt a knot form in my stomach. That really hurt me that my teacher had asked Lavinia and didn't include me in that invitation to play. Maybe she felt she had to do different things for her different students so each one would feel worthy. I mean, I was happy that Lavinia had something special, but this had nothing to do with her. It was the way I was perceived by my teacher that was the issue. You always have moments where you feel you're only as good as your last performance. So maybe my last performance for Ms. Liebling wasn't as good as she would have liked, and she figured she'd send someone else to play for a change. Regardless of the motive, it hurt any way.

"You know, you should tell your mom how you feel. She doesn't play an instrument; maybe she doesn't understand how subjective music is. One teacher or conductor will love you, the next one thinks your bow is too heavy or too light. One thinks you interpret Mozart brilliantly, another says you have no clue where the piece is going. You think anybody has the definitive right to tell you whether or not you've got the correct interpretation? It's our job to find our own voice. Sometimes that voice is outside the realm of what's accepted. If you audition for someone who has very set ideas about how your piece should sound, and your performance doesn't fit the bill, he's gonna' reject you. That doesn't mean you don't have great talent. It just means he is stuck in an interpretive rut."

"Yeah, well, either way I don't make the program. Joey, I don't know what I'll do if she takes away my violin. I don't know what I'll do? What would you do?"

"Whoa, that's a question I don't belong answering. I think you need to communicate better with your mom. I'm sure she knows how upset you'd be."

"She doesn't care. Communicate? That's a joke.

Our communication is limited to how many hours I can squeeze in today, and how straight my bow was throughout, or how flat the hair was on the bow during the Adagio. How tired are you or how are you feeling comes in last place in my house. She won't make the investment anymore if I'm not considered the best, Joey. My life is going to be a living hell for the next year till I audition again. And if I don't get in? . . . No way, I have to have a plan; and I have to make it now. I can't just let life happen to me anymore. You don't get it. You have a mother who actually loves you more than she loves the art."

"Oh, Lavinia come on, your mother loves you so much. Her every thought is you."

"Wrong. Her every thought is *about* me. Her every thought is the music, and where will I go with it? You don't know. Every time someone around here succeeds in something, I end up having the worst night of my life. I hear about it all night. 'Why wasn't it you? Why weren't you picked? You lazy girl. You not good enough.'"

"Really? Well, I understand her being envious of what other kids have achieved. That's normal. But she knows how talented you are and she knows you're not lazy. You'll make it."

"Thanks. I'll figure something out. She's not gonna' stop me, you'll see."

"Okay. Well, I've gotta get home. See ya next week."

"Bye, Joey Cohen. I'll see ya."

I had no idea how she was going to remedy this situation at home. I was just glad it wasn't my situation. Something inside me was very concerned about her. How many Lavinias were there in the classical music world? Probably more than any of us can imagine.

CHAPTER 12

BREAKDOWN

The Conservatory's big concerto competition was looming—now twelve weeks away. We were all working our fingers to the bone, literally. If you won, you got to play as the soloist with the top orchestra at American Institute. It was a big honor. I know this may sound odd, but I found myself thinking of Lavinia often. What would happen to her if she didn't win? How would she take the news? Even more importantly, how would her mother take the news? The possibilities sent shivers down my spine. I threw them off and kept working.

Each day I went to school, came home at 12:00 P.M., had lunch, and worked on my concerto. I had a snack, and worked on my concerto; took a 15 minute break, then Uncle Mischa and I would work on my concerto some more. By 7:30 P.M., I'd finish working on my concerto, then I'd eat dinner and do homework. Then I'd go to sleep, get up and do it all over again—for twelve weeks.

These were not the best of times! Especially since I had just moved to a new place and had begun a new school. Any time I had a major concert or media engagement, my life became agony for a couple of months. But I didn't necessarily want kids in my new school to know that about me, yet. They'd think I was some kind of nerd; they wouldn't understand that's just what a musician has to do. While they're spending a couple of hours a weekend on travel soccer teams, I'm practicing and running to long rehearsals everyday of the week. I had to put in the hours. I had to study for school exams. I had to complete homework assignments and projects on time. There was no one in my life saying, "Oh poor Joey, he's a concert violinist and gets all kinds of media attention, so let's go lightly on him this week." No . . . no one ever says that. One afternoon I had had it.

I threw my music books up against the wall (you always hurt the ones you love!) "I can't do this! I'm not going to make it. It's too much!" I screamed. I guess I needed my uncle to hear me. I guess I needed the whole world to hear me. Without missing a beat, he was in my room.

"What is it, Joey? Is it all too hard for you today?"

"Yeeeesssss!" I growled. I was sick of being in control. I was allowed to get out of control once in awhile, wasn't I?

"I know what you're going through. I remember how hard it was."

"You don't know. You didn't have all this work on top of competing. They give sooo much more work at school now than they used to. There are all these stupid standardized tests they try to prepare you for. It's never ending assignments. Even the teachers are stressed. You didn't have that!"

I was feeling pretty self righteous. The only thing that gave away my act of bravado was the steady stream of tears rolling down my cheeks.

"You're right. It wasn't this difficult to follow a dream when I was your age. There was more time for creativity and day dreaming. Of course, while other kids were day dreaming, I was practicing. Ha! But I have some funny stories to tell you. You'll see, come sit with me a minute." Uncle Mischa took a tissue out of his pocket and handed it to me.

"You know, once, when I was around your age, I was practicing the *Mendelssohn Concerto* for a competition. I complained and complained that I didn't want to put in all the hours. I was making your grandma absolutely crazy. I yelled, I screamed, I slammed doors, broke pencils—you name it. And what did she do? Another mother would have yelled back. Another mother would have told me to go to bed without dinner, or worse, without dessert. Another mother would have grounded me for a month. But no, my mother proceeded to take all the underwear out of my drawers and hurl them across my room. Then she grabbed my pajamas and T-shirts and hurled them to the far reaches of my desk. She'd look at me coolly and say, "Now put them back." She'd stand there until I refolded every last item—even my underwear. "You either put in the time your teacher said you need, or you'll be folding underwear for the whole family! Which do you choose, Mischa?" I chose practice.

Mischa loved to tell these stories, and they definitely alleviated the pain of practice.

"One time your grandma sent me to the neighborhood barber to get a haircut. She specifically made the appointment 15 days before a big concert I had to do, because she knew that was the amount of time it took for my hair to look—according to my mother—perfect.

It was the first time she sent me by myself. I was 11.
I returned home, opened the door and asked, "So, do
you like my haircut?"

"No," was her reply. "Will it grow back in time for
the concert?"

"No," was my reply. "It's a special kind of haircut.
It gets shorter and shorter." My mother was not
amused."

I was, though. I had really grown to love Uncle
Mischa. He left my room, seeming somehow satisfied
that he had helped me cope. But the heaviness I felt
in my chest, and the churning in my stomach did not
respond to Mischa's stories. The pressures were just
getting too great. I couldn't quite make my muscles
respond the way I wanted. The music I was making at
that moment was just not enough. Maybe music was-
n't enough at all anymore? I didn't want to end up like
Mischa, or Lavinia, or Noah, who had been beaten
down so many times he didn't remember what it felt
like to succeed. I didn't want to be swallowed up in
practice from morning until night. I couldn't get
Catherine to see me in any other light than "Bobby
Brady." Was I supposed to keep pining away for someone who was more connected to a clueless fourteen
year old violinist than a skydiver is to his chute? I
shut my score and started my homework. It was a
welcomed relief.

The next day in school, everything looked a little
different to me. I noticed things more: the groups of
boys joking and jostling each other around outside
the classrooms, the girls passing smiles to their
momentary objects of affection, the sounds of life that
had absolutely no connection to mine. I was minding

my own business, stuffing oversized math and social studies text books into my locker when I was approached, rather surprisingly, by two of the most popular girls in my grade, Tasha and Taryn. You had to love the names. They ranked, in my mind, right up there with Muffy and Bunny—some Manhattan favorites. Anyway, the conversation went something like this:

"So, Joey, you doing another concert this weekend, or you going out?"

"Well," I started carefully, "I'll be practicing, but no, I don't have a concert. I honestly don't know what I'll be doing yet. It's only Wednesday."

I hadn't minded the anonymity at Southbury so much, but here, in Manhattan, at a tense moment in my career as a teen, I had begun to mind it a lot.

"Oh, well you have to make plans by Wednesday, you know. All the good girls are taken by then for the weekend parties. Do you have one?"

"What—a girl or a party?" I asked naively.

"A girl, silly. To take to Hugh's party."

"I didn't even know Hugh was having a party."

"Oh Josef, you really have got to get out more." Tasha and Taryn sighed deeply and simultaneously. It must be in the genes—that sighing thing.

"Well, am I invited?" *Not that I really wanted to go, but I thought I wanted to go and that's what's important here.*

"Sure, come. No one ever sees you around unless it's on the news or a talk show. The kids don't know what to make of you. Are you a snob or a cool kid? Are you just uninterested in socializing? That wouldn't be normal, would it?"

"Uh, no, of course not." I wasn't sure exactly what they were driving at, but I didn't care at the moment. A few weeks ago, I would have said, "Nice talking to ya, but I've got class." Not this time. I wanted to know what it was like with them. I needed to know.

"So yeah, I'll come. Give me the time."

"Awesome! Saturday night, 8:00 P.M. Should we find you a date, or do you have one?"

Uh oh, this could be extremely bad, I thought. The truth is, though, I didn't have a date. I sure wasn't asking Catherine. She'd think I'd lost my marbles, or worse, my priorities. Anyway, my luck—just as I'd go to ask her, a swarm of tuba players would come marching down the hallway playing a classical rendition of *Swanee* (led by Gabriel on strings!), and that would be the end of that! Nope, I could handle this on my own.

"Yeah, you can fix me up with a date."

"All right. We'll make sure she's lots of fun," they giggled.

I closed my locker and went off to class—very pleased with my transaction.

Within one period, all the kids in the popular group at school seemed to know I'd be attending the Saturday night shindig at Hugh's. You know when there's a buzz going around school. It's actually palpable. You can feel the words tingling in the hallway, in the corners by the lockers, across the aisles in English class.

"Hey, Joey, see ya Saturday! Party!"

"Yeah, we hooked you up already. She is so hot!"

"Oh yeah? Great. Who is it?"

"See ya Saturday. You'll find out!"

Why wouldn't they tell me who? I had no idea what I was in for; yet I was uncharacteristically curious. It's not as if I had nothing else to occupy my time. The competition was breathing down my neck and school was keeping me pretty busy these days between an English report, science labs, and numerous tests a week.

Socially, though, I didn't exactly have distractions. Kids in school were all still on the verge of getting to know me—sniffing me out. They were trying to figure out what I do, where I've been, and what media I've been publicized in. You see, the kids in Manhattan love to be around "stars." They were still trying to figure out if I was one.

In Manhattan, they're very impressed if you've made a name for yourself in anything, as opposed to in my old town, where the more anonymous you were, the easier it was to keep the peace. Kids strove for anonymity: You didn't want to be looked at too much in class and at recess, you wanted to be a tree, be a scratching post, be anything but worthy of notice. Needless to say, it was not so easy for me there.

But God Bless Manhattan—home of the soon to be's and has beens. You either are on your way to becoming a star or you have a parent who was, but now they're washed up and they spend their time coming to classes on parent-career day and talking about acting, singing, dancing, making music, writing, modeling—the demise of their youth, the fascinating careers they highly don't recommend young people get involved in.

"Don't get sucked into it children," they'd always say, "in the end it'll swallow you up."

Once the kids mark you as "valuable" they begin the invitations. They invite you to parties you can't attend (for fear of police raids), study sessions where no studying gets done, and Sunday brunches where brunch isn't really one of the activities on the menu. They're looking for trouble, excitement, anyone else's life but their own. I have already noticed there's a lot of that going on.

If you're on your way, been on TV, in the papers; you're hot—a commodity—someone to know. They follow you around, hoping to catch a draft from your coattails on the way up. You're supposed to decide if they're worth the trouble of friendship in the two or three free hours you possess in a week. That decision alone can take up a great deal of time. It's like having a preponderance of static on your phone line. You hang on and listen for a minute or so and then you hang up because there's no one on the other end, and you can't waste anymore time. Time during youth is way too precious for just hanging on. Well, that's kind of like school in Manhattan. Lots of noise and static.

CHAPTER 13

LIFE OF THE PARTY

So Saturday night came. I took out my staple "going out clothes"—a black v-neck sweater, white undershirt, and khaki pants; checked out the hair, a little gel, a determined stare into the mirror—yep, I was ready.

I pocketed Hugh's address and took the subway up to the East 70's. His building was obviously doorman friendly—there were three of them. I didn't know who to look at to inquire about the party. But somehow they all knew where I was headed.

"Mr. Hugh Montgomery's apartment, sir?" They all bowed and asked simultaneously.

"Uh, yes. I don't know the floor."

"Penthouse suite, sir."

"Whoa . . . I mean, thank you."

I took the elevator to the 25th floor. I walked out onto a dark green and black marble floor, with walls of deep cherry. This was something else. The doors were opened and music was blaring from the living room. There were about 12 couples from what I could see—only two people above 5'2"; however, they were on their way out as I was coming in. Hugh came to greet me.

"Joey, glad you could come. What a bore these parties are without different types, you know?"

All that was missing from his opening was "old chap."

"Yeah, sure, I know what you mean."

"Well, come on and have a drink from the bar."

"From the bar? No, that's okay. I'm not really thirsty."

"Who has to be thirsty?" Hugh laughed and continued, "No one here is thirsty. I bet you can't wait to meet your date, huh?"

He was right about that. I figured I better be in full control of my senses if I was going to meet whoever they picked out for me. Hugh beckoned to someone sitting on the couch, and over she strutted—a blonde girl in a low cut white angora sweater. She certainly was great looking. But she hadn't opened her mouth yet, so the jury was still out on her personality.

"Joey, this . . . is . . . the one, the only, Honey."

He took such time introducing her I thought he was trying to sell her to me. Honey didn't say much, she just snapped her gum and eyed me, like a cat eyes a mouse

"Hi Honey. I'm Joey."

"I know who you are. I watched you on all the talk shows. You're like . . . somebody, aren't you?" she said, moving closer.

"Uh, no . . . no. I'm a violinist, but I'm an 8th grader like you."

"Get me something to drink, okay Joey."

"Ah sure," I said. She didn't look like the root beer type. I went over toward the bar and noticed that each couple at this party was slowly ascending the winding staircase disappearing into different rooms. This wasn't like any party we gave in Southbury. Where were they going? The food and music was down here. Within minutes there was no one left in the living room but us. I used my imagination. Quickly. I got my date a spritzer, the most innocuous drink I could think of, and thought about what I could do with her. I just met her, she snapped her gum, and her name was Honey. I was desperate for divine intervention. As I thought, my hand stumbled through my pocket over some crumpled paper. These were the pants I wore on the train coming to the city. I was still carrying around Greg's phone number. That was it—the brainstorm I'd been looking for. She was a girl looking for adventure, and I was a boy looking for an "out." I'd call Greg. Maybe we could double date or do something cool down in No Ho.

Since there was no one around at the moment, I helped myself to the phone at the bar and called the number.

"Hey Greg, is that you?"

"Yeah, who is this?"

"I don't know if you remember me, I'm the violinist you met on the train coming to the city."

"Hey, yeah, Joey, right? How's life?"

"Uh, great, listen I was wondering . . ."

"You wanna' come to a party tonight at my sister's loft?"

"Actually, that sounds cool. Can I bring a date?"

"Excellent, the more the merrier. Come on over. I'll tell ya all about life in the Ho's!"

"What?"

"The No Ho's! You still have my address?"

"Yep, right here."

"Okay. See ya later."

Well, that was easy. I returned to Honey.

"Honey, how would you like to split and go to a party down in NOHO."

"Mmmm, sounds dangerous . . . let's do it."

"Dangerous? It's NOHO, you know, near SOHO."

"Okay, Okay, let's GoHO."

We had no goodbyes to say because the host and the rest of his guests had disappeared behind cherry wood doors. So, we left.

We hopped in a cab at the corner of 72nd St.

"So who are your teachers this year?" I asked, hoping to begin a meaningful conversation.

"Morel for French, Garrish for science, Mosley for soc, Hubert for English and, I don't even remember who I have for math. I go as infrequently as possible!" She laughed and snapped her gum out the window.

"Oh, so did you have that English test yesterday in Hubert's class?"

"Yeah. What was he thinking, giving a six paragraph essay test in forty minutes?"

"I know, I barely got to the closing, and I was writing a hundred miles an hour."

"I barely got to the second, and I couldn't care less. Nothing counts till high school anyway. Why do you care?" She had this middle school female look of disgust on her face, as if to say, "How dense are you?"

"Well, I care. I want to get into the best dual college/conservatory program I can. If you don't start making things count now, it's harder to do well later."

Uh oh, I was preaching. Not good, not good at all. You have to be cool, nonchalant, like nothing matters. I can do that. Let's see . . .

"But, you know, you're probably right. You can hang out a lot more with your friends if you don't spend so much time on work."

"Exactly. We all just see you blowing in and out of school every day, on your way to some rehearsal, with a layover in English class. You have to be in a group in school, you know, to get to the best parties and know the best people."

"Oh."

"Yeah, like Hugh. He makes a big bash every weekend. You're never at those. And Robbie takes a group out to Starbucks every Wednesday night, to celebrate over the hump."

"Really? How many?"

"Oh, about twenty or twenty-five kids. He doesn't worry about grades or money. All his dad has to do is throw a few million at Harvard for a new wing, and he's in."

"But Robbie's not a good student."

"Exactly! Now you're catching on. This isn't Southbury, Joey, it's Manhattan. Different things do the talkin' around here. So anyway, what do you think of Trish? Everybody has the hots for her."

"Well, she's okay."

"Okay? You must be the only guy who thinks that. She's the bomb of 8th grade. I'm dying to get invited to her Spring Fling. Everybody who matters goes. Taryn and Trisha, Hugh, Bobby, Marco, Jed, Emily, Ashley, you know the ones. The invitations will be going out next week. Ooh, I'll have to go shopping."

A wave of nausea came over me. I never even talked to half these people. I used to think it was a waste of time. I'd never have time to hang with them anyway, right? And they'd just make me feel badly about having goals and different perspectives from them. They'd never understand. Those grapes were sour anyway. I didn't speak much for the rest of the cab ride. I was serenaded by the popping of gum and tapping of freshly manicured silk wraps on the window ledge.

Twenty minutes later we arrived at the loft. It wasn't exactly as I expected. A very drab gray building with fire escapes running up the sides. It looked more like a factory than a home. The number was almost totally scratched off the heavy metal door at the side of the building, but I could hear from the music blaring out of the top floor that we were at the right place. I rang the buzzer. A mop of disheveled, spiked hair stuck out from the upstairs window—and it had a voice!

"Hey man, I'll ring ya in, come on up!"

"Hi Greg, thanks."

We entered an old gated elevator that creaked and complained all the way up to the top floor. As I pushed open the gates I saw a huge space, covered—from floor to ceiling —with art and people. There had to be 100 kids packed into this loft; paintings and sculptures everywhere. There was a sculpture of a glossy, white toilet seat in the middle of the room. I asked Greg what they call it; he said, "Glossy White Toilet Seat." Next to the kitchen was a ten-foot-long piece of pointillism, drop cloths all over the floors with color combinations I've never seen before, and a tiny kitchen tucked away in the far right corner, near the window.

Greg explained that his sister, the artist, and her roommates went out for the night. It was just a bunch of 14 year olds, Honey and me. He looked so different to me from the young, idealistic boy I had met on the train. He was wearing a black T-shirt, black sleeveless ski vest, and ripped black jeans (the color of the city). His hair was spiked and very purposefully unkempt.

"Oooh, he's cute, Joey. How do you know him?"

"Uh, I met him on a train. I've done a lot of traveling, you know . . . because of my musical career," I added desperately, trying to impress her and bring her back my way!

"Really? So does Greg live here or is he visiting?"

"He's just spending the year here with his sister who's an artist."

"Fascinating. Is he hooked up?"

"What exactly do you like about Greg?!" I snapped, becoming extremely annoyed.

"Well, what's not to like? He's wild looking and he lives without parents in a loft in NOHO . . . very mature . . . dangerous even. I love it . . . Does he drive?"

"HE'S FOURTEEN!"

"Oh . . . he looks much older—so tall, you know?"

Okay, I had to take charge here. I could be wild and dangerous too. Oh yeah, just ask anyone. I was a regular George of the Jungle! "So you wanna' dance?"

"I'd like a drink. Can you be a lamb and get me one?"

Hmmm . . . I said George of the Jungle, not the Farm! "Sure, what would you like?"

"Some of that punch looks really yummy."

So I was a gentleman and filled up her glass. I

poured myself some as well. Honey definitely responded differently to me after she finished that drink. I was
feeling pretty happy myself. What was in that stuff? I
started sweating and feeling a bit light headed.

"Honey, is all the paint thinner in this loft affecting
you? I'm getting a little dizzy."

"Ha! That's just 'cause you can't hold your liquor,
Joe-sy."

Joe-sy? Where did that come from? "You mean
that punch was spiked?" I asked incredulously. After
all, we were underage.

"Oh, you're such a prude Joey Cohen."

Obviously my first name didn't have enough sylla-
bles with which to make her point.

"Listen, bring me over to meet Greg. I'll be your
best friend, K?"

"K...I mean okay." I gave in. My head was spinning
and I was in no mood to argue. Just what I needed,
another friend who was a girl.

"And get me another one of those awesome punch-
es."

"No. You know what, Honey? I don't think you
should have anymore. You're gonna' get really sick."

"Josef, what I'm gonna' get is really happy. This is
part of the social scene. Get with it, or get lost."

What a snob, I thought. I wasn't gonna' help her
get drunk and pass out. Let her get it herself.

"Look, if you want to party like that, go ahead, but
it's not my thing and I don't want to feel responsible if
something happens to you. I'll be happy to introduce
you to Greg though."

"Well then, I'll get my own drink. Let's go meet the
hunk."

So Honey swept by the punch table, filled up her tank, and excitedly walked over with me to talk to Greg.

"Greg, Honey would like to meet you," I said gallantly.

"Oh, hey . . . nice to meet you—Honey, is it?"

"Ha! Yeah! That's me!" She laughed flirtatiously.

"What school do you guys go to . . . Honey (he pronounced her name with extreme emphasis and delight, as if he was enjoying the taste of a Crème Brule), and what grade are you in?"

"I'm in 8th at Lincoln Middle."

"8th—excellent."

Greg turned to me and asked in a whisper, "So, are you two together, or can I . . .?"

"Oh no, be my guest. She's not my girlfriend," I responded with a measure of relief.

"Wow . . . great . . . she is hot!!" Greg effused.

"Oh yeah—hot, hot, hot, plenty hot," I blushed and chanted in mantra like fashion. This was the kind of girl who could definitely burn me!

Greg smirked, ran his fingers through his spiky, gelled hair, turned back toward Honey and transformed into Mr. Machismo. "So Honey," he continued, "what do you do for fun in this big, bad city?"

"Well, I like movies, shopping, going out to dinner—actually going out for lunch isn't bad either. A bunch of us just tried that little Italian place in the village on Bleeker that just opened. It was amazing!"

"Is that the one that's downstairs in the basement of an old townhouse . . . Volare's or something?"

"Yeah, yeah, yeah . . . that's the place. Were you there? With the jazz music and the oversized portions.

We loved that place!"

"Yep, I just went with a group of friends last night.
It was a blast."

Wow, I thought, *he was out last night and tonight
he has a party. Not only that, Greg had a group of
friends and he's only been in the city as long as I have.
I'm definitely doing something wrong here. Is it me, or
is it that I have barely enough time to sleep, let alone
talk to kids my own age?*

"Sounds like fun," swooned Honey. "Did you see
that last *Lord of the Rings* yet?"

"Yep."

"Was it awesome or what? Four or five of us went
last weekend, then we hit Peppermint Park for sun-
daes. It's on the Upper West Side. Did you ever go?"

"Peppermint Park is the best!" Blurted Greg enthu-
siastically.

Oh, they were made for each other.

"Did you ever have their Mile High Mud Pie? Whoa.
Sometimes I cut class with my friends before lunch
and go uptown to have it. What a sugar rush!"

"You do that? Awesome!"

TIRESOME! I couldn't listen to this anymore. I felt
like an immigrant right off the boat from Putsville. I
had never heard of any of these places, and I hadn't
been to a movie since I left Southbury. Not to mention
the fact that I felt totally excluded. My date for the
evening had dumped me and was mooning over a guy
I had met on a train, who thought he was a writer and
wore ripped up jeans, had delusions of Bohemia, and
a glossy, white toilet seat in the middle of his living
room. This was not my scene—even if I wanted it to
be. Who was I kidding?

"Uh, guys? . . ."

By this time they were looking deeply into each other's eyes with "great expectations," dreaming of mud pies and Gandolf.

"I hate to break this up, but I'll be leaving now."

No response. Honey was looking very unsteady on her feet. I don't know why, but I was worried about her. I went to get my coat, pushing my way through the throngs of street-wise souls, stomping to the beat of the electric monster mounted on the wall. This was a normal Saturday night. This was a life lesson.

By the time I returned with my coat to say goodbye to Greg, Honey was splayed out on the couch, snoring her way deep into "punch" heaven. I saw that one coming. I found Greg, thanked him for the invite and he thanked me for the intro.

"Honey is . . .(I knew what was coming) AWE-SOME!"

"Yeah. . . .see ya Greg."

"I'll call ya. We'll catch a movie."

"Sure."—Not.

The music splattered in the air like the pointillism framed on his walls. I left.

I thought I'd feel better about things by morning, but I didn't. I felt betrayed and strangely alone—I had never experienced those particular feelings before. I always felt safe in my world of popping strings and overachieving instrumentalists. Sunday was all a depressing blur. Before I knew it, it was Monday morning. and I went to school. At the first bell, I saw Hugh and Taryn in the hallway.

"Hey!" I said.

Ignored.

What was that about? A bunch of kids were huddled by the lockers as I passed. One of them was Honey. What was I supposed to do, ignore her?

"Hi Honey."

"Oh, it's Joey virtuoso. Whad' ya do for the rest of the weekend? Stay home and listen to smart music?"

The whole crowd erupted in laughter. I couldn't believe this was going to be my life now. I didn't know what to say.

"Yeah, Honey, that's exactly what I did. But I'm glad to see you've come out of your coma." I moved on as quickly as possible.

At 12:20 P.M. I left the school and headed toward A.I.M. for my lesson with Ms. Liebling. I was not looking forward to this. I'd been having trouble concentrating on my concerto for two weeks now, without knowing why. But today, I had a perfectly good reason. The problem was, I couldn't tell Ms. Liebling about it. It was way too big, and she was always way too busy. The streets and cars all whizzed by me as I walked. There was no difference between them. I entered the lobby at A.I.M. unconsciously, went to the elevator and pushed 4. When I got off, I could see Ms. Liebling's door open; she was waiting for me.

"Ah, schatsy, how is it going?"

Of course I knew she meant the concerto. Forget how it was going with me! I had become the sum total of movements in a Bruch Concerto.

"Oh, just fine," I lied.

"Good, good, sweetheart. Come by the piano and let's start because I must finish exactly on time today. I have a competition to judge."

"Sure, Ms. Liebling."

I began to play. Before I knew it, I had finished the first movement and was into the second. I remembered thinking how odd it was for Ms. Liebling not to stop me at all with comments. But, I just went on my way and barreled through into the third movement. When I was done there was silence. Ms. Liebling was just staring at me with her arms folded. *Say something,* I thought to myself. I stood in silence before my teacher.

"Joey, you have to play this for the competition when?"

"In three weeks," I answered, knowing full well that she knew when that competition was.

"I think you should sit down, Joey."

I wasn't prepared for another serious event in my life. I was really just barely making it through the last one.

"Joey, we have to talk, you and I. If this is the way you have prepared the concerto for me today, I think maybe you should consider taking a break from violin after the competition. I mean, it hasn't been up to your usual level for two weeks; your intonation was off, you were no where inside the piece. I felt nothing. The bow was too light. Your dynamics were nonexistent. I think you need to consider whether this is something you want to stick with."

"What? The concerto or violin?"

"Violin, my dear. It happens sometimes that young, prodigious talents burn out. You may be a little burnt out. Or you may have decided, unconsciously, that you really don't want this. After all, it takes you away from your social life, sports, your home. Maybe you're rebelling without even knowing it."

Her words sunk into my chest like the winning blow of a knight's lance. I couldn't respond, so she continued.

"You know, to keep up the level of intensity and success you've been going at, you need to devote even more time. You're still quite young, but the older you get the more vital it becomes to put in the hours and detail work. I don't think you really want to be doing this now. You have to come to a decision."

She wouldn't stop talking. My head was swimming.

"Of course you have to make it through your next competition, but after that, I want you to take some time to think. You know, I have my name riding on you, schatsy. I can't just let you play any old way. You have to have things organized; even your sentiment must be organized."

I spoke. "But sentiment can't be organized. That would be contrived. You feel what you feel when you feel it."

"Yes dear, but you have to have the ideas about how you're going to emote each section before you get up and 'feel' it. Otherwise you have a very risky performance. It can't all happen on the spur of a moment."

I was going to implode—just be sucked up in some cosmic vacuum and disappear—me and my violin. I never had issues about playing. I knew what I wanted. I was devoted. Why wasn't anything coming out right?

"You really need to examine your future Joey. I really mean it. Now let's get to work on some of the details, okay?"

I couldn't concentrate. I might as well have gone home. I stood there for the rest of the hour and attempted to do what Ms. Liebling suggested. I think after about 15 minutes she had just given up on me and was marking time on the clock till the end of the lesson. Mercifully, it ended.

"Bye, Ms. Liebling."

"Bye, Joey. Remember what I said."

Remember? It was etched on the wave of nausea billowing in my stomach. Maybe it was true. I had nothing else in me. Washed up at 13. I had to talk to someone. I went home. Luckily Uncle Mischa was out in the living room when I got back.

"Why the long face, Joey?" He asked.

"I just had the worst lesson of my life. Uncle Mischa, did your teacher ever tell you that you were washed up?"

"What? No, of course not. I mean, I had some lessons that I wouldn't want to crow about, but no, even Pedagogia never said that. Did Ms. Liebling say that to you?"

"Well, not in so many words, but she intimated that I should think of giving up violin."

"What? Utter nonsense! You had a bad lesson, so what?"

"No, it's more than that. She says I've sounded empty for two weeks, and when that happens it's a sign."

"It's a sign that you should stop playing? No, it's a sign that you're feeling empty. That happens. You're thirteen . . . lots on your mind . . . loaded with homework and tests . . . puberty . . . unrequited loves . . . everyone goes through that at some point. Does that

155

mean they all stop playing? No. You must show her and rise to the occasion. You're just in a slump. You know, like a batter or pitcher. They don't throw the batter off the team because he can't hit well for a few weeks or even months."

Mischa was steaming. I could see this really got to him. His past must have overtaken him for a moment.

"I know what's inside you. Your parents and grandmother know what's inside you. She's only with you a couple of hours a week. How can she make such a call?"

"I don't know. She's Ms. Liebling. She knows."

"But what do you know, Joey? Do you know that the music has left you? Can you stand there and look me in the eye and say it's gone. Tell me, Joey. Look me in the eye and say it!" Mischa's voice rang through the walls with the anger of years. He was as enraged as I've ever seen him.

"Come. Come to the window." He threw open the pane. "Do you hear it, Joey? Do you hear the music? Listen to the city. Lincoln Center. The fountain . . . the violinists from the Philharmonic keeping step across the plaza with the beat of their hearts . . . the hopeful, young soloists rehearsing in an empty Avery Fischer . . . the echo of their strings resound and mingle with those of artists long gone—comforting each other as they disappear into time together . . . the years of joyous toil, all for a moment of critical acclaim. Answer me, Josef Cohen. Is that music still in you, child? . . . ANSWER ME!"

I was shaking. I didn't know what to say. But I believed that if I opened my mouth, the right thing would come out, so I did. "I don't want to give up,

Uncle Mischa. It's still there. The music . . . it's still there." The words burst from my mouth like tears after the floodgates have been opened.

"Because you know you can do it, isn't that right, Joey?"

"Yes. I know I can do it."

"There's an old story my teacher once told me about a village full of broken clocks. One day a miracle worker came and found he could repair only one."

"Which one, Uncle Mischa?" I sniffled.

"The one that had been wound faithfully every day by its owner. You see, Joey, if you stay engaged, and keep working the music every day, with great intent and faithfulness, something will spark once again, and you'll feel it. Your music hasn't gone anywhere, my boy—you have." His smile wrapped me in hope.

"I can do it, Uncle Mischa," I reiterated softly.

Was it really as simple as that? I heard myself say the words, but could I make them real? I would work very hard now. My uncle told me I had reason to— because I could—because the city was listening. I wasn't so sure anybody was listening.

CHAPTER 14

THE COMPETITION

The A.I.M. competition was a big musical event in our neighborhood. A.I.M. made the competition opened seating in the audience, so the neighborhood kids could attend and watch the competitors. They felt it was an experience for non-conservatory kids to see a slice of life they may never know otherwise. So, posters for the event were mounted in all the neighborhood schools. Mine was no exception. There were photos and bios of the major contenders—each with their competition time slot. I was the only performer from our school. These posters were put up in every hallway, and every time I walked past one I heard muffled laughter from huddled masses of students, hanging around the corridors. As the last bell rang and the corridors cleared I saw why. Every one of my photos had been defaced—complete with devil ears, blackened teeth and insults:

"VIOLIN FREAK," "NERD," "LOSER," . . .

Voices . . . "Oh Joey, I can't wait to hear you play. I'll be there, hon," purred Ashley. "I'LL BRING ABSOLUTELY EVERYBODY! . . . NOT!!!" she exploded in laughter along with the other nameless five girls in her cadre.

"Yeah, Joey, I'll get the whole basketball team

down. Wouldn't want to miss this!" Ryan yelped and turned toward his cohorts. "Violin boy!"

"Don't worry, Joey, we'll all be in the audience. Wouldn't want you to CHOKE or anything!" Melissa crowed and swung her pony tail across my face as she left.

"Gee, thanks for the support, guys. I really appreciate that."

I felt like less than nothing. Their derision was unbearable. How could I have achieved so much in my thirteen years and be made to feel like less than nothing in a few surreal minutes? All day I walked the hallways from class to class being pointed at, laughed about, and generally harassed.

I had to contain my tears. I couldn't let them see they had gotten to me. Even the toughest of them had to have felt humiliated at some time. They must know what they're doing to me. What did I ever do to them? They don't even know me. They think they do. But they have no clue. I could be just like them. If I didn't play the violin . . . I could be just like them. I was good in sports, but they'd never know it. I liked to hang out as much as the next kid, but they'd never think to include me. Well, if they did, I guess I wouldn't have much time any way. THIS IS BULL! WHY AM I DOING THIS?

The weeks passed, and somehow I woke up each day and got through practice and going to school. I was as ready as I was ever going to be for that competition. My time slot was 10:40 A.M. on Saturday, April 14th. We arrived at American Institute of Music in plenty of time—at 10:00 A.M. My uncle had reserved a practice room for me a week ahead of time, and we marched right up to the second floor to begin warming up. The only problem was that Luba was not in the building yet. Mischa always asked Luba to arrive a half hour early for rehearsals, concerts, competitions, etc. because Luba had to come from Brooklyn and there was often terrible traffic getting to us in Manhattan, and terrible parking problems in the city. Either way spells possible disaster if you don't leave plenty of time to get to your destination. Today was a competition, it was now 10:10 A.M. and Luba was not yet at A.I.M., but I wasn't worried. I didn't have to be. Mischa said that was his job. I've got to tell you, by 10:20, my uncle was plenty worried.

"Okay, look Joey," he said in his best "I've got it together" tone, "if Luba doesn't make it, you'll have to either play with whatever accompanist they have around, or you'll have to perform a capella (without accompaniment). Just be ready for whatever comes. You're a pro. You can do it."

As Mischa was talking I could see he was trying to convince himself as well.

"I'm going to run downstairs and see if Luba is looking for us." Mischa left like a bolt of lighting leaving the sky—fast and loud, slamming the door behind him. I just continued warming up. He was back up in less than five minutes.

"We've got to get downstairs. Luba is nowhere to be found, and you have to be on time for your slot. It's almost 10:30, let's go. Just remember, go with it, whatever it is. My uncle carried himself with the certainty of experience.

We took the elevator down to the main hall. As we rounded the corner we saw Lavinia's mother walking toward us. Just who I wanted to see before a competition.

"Ah, I saw your accompanist about fifteen minutes ago looking around for you in the lobby."

"You did?" my uncle queried. "Well what happened to her? She never came up to the practice room."

"Oh, I told her to just wait for you at the hall because that's what all the other accompanists were doing. They were waiting for the kids to finish their warm ups and meet them at the hall."

"You told her to meet us at the hall?" My uncle's ears were turning purple. "But I asked her yesterday to meet us at the practice room I had reserved. That was the whole point of getting her here early, so they could rehearse together. They hadn't had time this week. This was going to be it before the competition."

"Well, I didn't know that," Lavinia's mom replied, turning redder by the minute.

"But why would you tell her where to meet us if you didn't know what our plans were? You didn't know what we had decided? Luba probably thought our plans had changed, and she listened to you. That wasn't right, what you did."

Oh boy, this was definitely not the time to get into a fist fight. I didn't think the judges would look kindly on that. Or perhaps, they've been judging instrumental competitions so long, they'd enjoy doing a blow-by-blow of two pre-college family members on the edge.

"This is getting us nowhere," my uncle admitted, "let's just forget about it."

"Forget about it, good idea" said Lavinia's mom relieved. She knew my uncle was right. She shouldn't have been meddling. One can hypothesize all day about whether or not that meddling was calculated, but it doesn't matter, because within seconds of resolving this Ms. Liebling. came skidding out of the hall on the heels of her shoes.

"Ach, schatsy what are you doing here? You need to be backstage, you're on, you're on."

"But it's only 10:30 A.M." I countered. "I have ten minutes to wait for Luba."

"Luba is backstage already. Where were you? She has been here for fifteen minutes."

"Yes, that's what we heard," said my uncle with great helpings of sarcasm in his voice."

"Well, you need to be back there now. They finished early with the last one—made minced meat of him. But they'll love you, schatsy, if you ever get on that stage!"

"Minced meat, huh? One thing about Ms. Liebling, she had a way of really calming you down before an important event!"

So I ran backstage, hugged Luba, made a swift entrance onto main-stage, bowed, and off we went. Well, off I went anyway. My first movement was a terrifyingly fast spiccato section (spiccato is a loose bouncing of the bow on the string, making it sound like little staccato notes), which, I guess because of all the adrenaline pumping in the teachers in my life prior to going on, came out faster than I had ever played it before. I kept feeling like I was one step away from falling off a cliff. Not an ideal sensation to have during a competition. I knew my accents and rhythm weren't absolutely perfect.

Why was I running so fast? I saw images before me—a face—it was my own . . . with devil's ears and

blackened teeth. I heard laughter, louder, more frequent, drowning me, rolling around in my head, in
between my ears. I must get through this. *STOP
LAUGHING AT ME. MAKE IT STOP.* I got to the calm of
the second movement. I breathed. Control at last.

The next two movements I nailed. I just felt like I
was in the zone. The violin became part of my body
and I felt my whole self just gliding through space—
the bow felt like silk in my hand. I was in total control, yet not aware of my body. It's the coolest feeling.
I was one with the instrument.

I finished my 3rd movement cadenza with a roar of
chords. I pulled my bow off the strings with a flourish
and left it suspended in the air just a little longer than
usual. Valery would have been so proud of me. I
bowed deeply, heard my applause, and left the stage.
In a flicker of an eye, a thing I gave up months of my
life for, was over. Isn't that the way it always is?

I was the last of my age group to play in the competition that morning. As I walked out of the hall I was
immediately surrounded by Catherine, Noah, Lavinia
and Gabe—one of Maestro Vunderfall's students, —
reportedly excellent, though I had never gotten a
chance to hear him perform. All I knew is that he
must be pretty good if Catherine had fallen for him. I
wanted to hate him. That feeling didn't come easily to
me. Couldn't do it. We were all within two years of
each other. Gabe was fourteen—just at the cut off age
for the competition. We were all too close in too many
ways to harbor bad feelings. We were, after all was
said and done, all we had.

"You were amazing!!" Catherine chirped. "No body
has more fire than you when you play, Joey. Where

does it come from? How do you summon that up?"

That was Catherine for you, always making me feel better about life. I felt like such a dog after having that experience with Honey—even though her sights were set elsewhere. But look, I might not have even gone looking for that experience if it weren't for Cat. She'd done me wrong! . . . Well, maybe not . . . I mean, she thought she was just being my friend, and friends can talk about anything. I never came out and told her how I felt. Maybe that was a mistake. Maybe even crossing the line was a mistake. Who knows!!! UGGGH! This bottled up feeling that was coming in my thirteenth year was not a good one.

I jumped right into the banter. "Forget that. Your legato is better than mine, Cat," I retorted.

"No, Joey, did you hear yourself up there? We don't stand a chance," Lavinia chimed in.

"What are you talking about? I deserved a speeding ticket up there for my first movement. I could feel Ms. Liebling twitching in the audience. This one is gonna' belong to one of you. I'm sure you guys were more consistent than I was today," I rebutted.

"You were incredible this morning too, Lavinia," added Catherine. "It's the best I've ever heard you play. And Gabe, my parents sat in on your audition this morning while I was warming up. They said you played the sweetest *Mendelssohn* they ever heard— dreamy, even."

Oh boy, I thought. She has got it bad!

"What about you, Catherine? I was in the audience for your audition, too. You were perfect. I mean there is nothing I could find wrong," Lavinia managed, (and believe me, compliments did not come easily to her).

I know this all sounds unbelievably saccharin, but this is one of two things that happen among participants after a competition. Either they make each other feel sublime, like they're the best thing since sliced bread (probably as a way to soften the blow, when they, themselves don't win), or they stand off in the corners—we call them the nether-reaches of the Institute's lobby—with their mothers, making no eye contact with anyone who could remotely be a rival.

"I'm really sorry I couldn't hear the three of you," I said earnestly, "I was busy freaking out over the whereabouts of my accompanist." They all laughed charitably.

So, the five of us nervously clotted in a huddle in the lobby. We must have looked like such a sight, encircling the bulletin board where, any minute, the results would go up. We could have taken seats on the couches, or gone down to wait in the cafeteria, or, like some of our cohorts, stashed ourselves into spurious corners of the lobby, staring at our feet. But no . . . there we were, the five expectants—waiting, jabbering, giggling nervously.

"You know," began Catherine, "when I was three and a half years old, I would drag all the pillows from the den couch into the middle of the living room floor. I'd arrange them before me in twos, one on top of the other, so they'd make a fluffy, square platform. Then I'd carefully step on them and inch my way over to the center, holding my tiny, 1/8 size violin in one hand and my bow in the other. As soon as I was sure of my footing, I'd place the violin under my chin, give a little bounce on the pillows, and start to play *Twinkle Variations and Lightly Row*. All the time I'd be pretending that the pillows were a grand stage and I was the evening's soloist. Sometimes I'd come out in my nightgown, the frillier the better, just so I could feel like I was in an evening gown. I still remember that." Catherine seemed very amused with her memory.

"My older brother used to taunt me. "You'll never play any concerts. You're such a dork, Cathy!"

"Mommmmmm!!" I'd scream, "Joshy called me a dork! Terrible thing—dork! Mean Joshy for saying dork! Bad Joshy for calling Cathy dork! What's a dork?! Then everyone in my family would fall down laughing."

"Well, you sure showed Joshy, didn't you?" I laughed supportively.

"Yeah, I guess. It's to be seen, right? You're only as good as your last performance."

"Oh, we get a little more latitude than that—because we're still young," I countered.

"No you don't. They start calling you inconsistent. I heard a judge say that about me once right in this school. It ruined my week. The worst part is, it puts you in a bad mood during regular school, and your friends try to find out why you're in a bad mood, and you tell them it's because some teacher at conservatory called you inconsistent. Try making them understand that! They think you're totally whacked!"

"Well, yeah, you don't expect friends from school to understand why that kind of comment might be devastating. How are they supposed to understand us at all? You don't live it—you don't get it." I felt strangely comfortable saying that now. This was my world, for better or worse.

"I don't really care what kids at school think of

me," sniffed Lavinia. "When you start expecting them to get what you're about, you're in for lots of disappointments."

"I care," Catherine added. "Our lives are exciting but I want to have a normal life with friendships and too much homework, and watching an occasional sitcom. You've gotta' have something else in your life."

"If you want to be the best, you've got to give up everything—suffer for your art," Lavinia pontificated.

"OOO, sounds ominous," joked Catherine.

"Look, you do what you can at the moment. You juggle your emotions with your responsibilities, and you try to keep the perspective that no competition is a life or death scenario. There's always another one and there's more to making you into a full artist than just music. Of course, it also helps to remember that the judges are human," I sermonized.

"Jes, and that they're probably wearing polka dotted underwear. That helps me mucho!!" Gabriel piped up.

Everyone laughed. Inside I was dying a little. What a fake I was. Here I'm preaching to a crowd of prodigies that they have to not take all this so seriously. That all you can do is your best and that there are other concerns in their lives; that this thing we do, this music monster, cannot take over. And what do I do? I stand in a hallway of fantastically talented young people, with waves of nausea wafting over me, biting my nails and promising God everything but my first born child, if He'll only let me win this competition. No matter what I do or say, it still means everything, doesn't it?

A skinny, red haired boy who I had seen around,

came walking over to the bulletin board with a paper in his hand. He glanced at us, trying to place our names, glanced at the paper and smiled. He took a thumb tack from his pocket and, with a flourish, put the paper up for all to see.

"Please tell me. Joey, tell me. I can't bear to look," Catherine whispered to me

"No, no, I've got to see for myself," snipped Lavinia, true to form.

Lavinia and I were neck and neck at that paper, and there it was in bold print:

Winner of the American Institute of Music Orchestral Competition:

Catherine Wohl

Second Place:

Gabriel Santos

Well . . . I failed. A cold sweat swept over me and covered me completely like the blankets they put over a car-wreck victim. My eyes fell on Lavinia. She was devastated, and I have to admit, as happy as I was for Catherine (yes, and even for Gabriel), that's how deeply I felt Lavinia's loss. It took me away from my own pain for a moment. Her eyes, her expression of sheer fear. What would she tell her mother?

It could have been any of us. Judging is so sub-jective. A particular preference in bow arm or vibrato speed could sway a judge and make or break a career. It could have been me—but I lost it . . . lost my focus . . . my edge. I let them all get to me.

"Catherine, I'm so happy for you. You really deserved it! You're on your way!" I said, holding back my giant wave of disappointment. I was so happy for her, though. She was a beautiful violinist. She was my friend.

"Gabriel, way to go. Congratulations."

"Thank you, Josef."

Lavinia got herself together, put on a brave face, and congratulated them. I could see a storm brewing inside. She walked down to the cafeteria to face her mother. Catherine and Gabriel went off to call their parents. *What was wrong with me? How could I let anybody take this from me?* I walked through the lobby in a daze. I heard someone suddenly calling my name. It was Ms. Liebling.

"Joey, darling. I'm glad I caught you. I wanted to talk."

"Hi Ms. Liebling. I'm so sorry I let you down. I really am."

"Sweetheart, look, you did your best. These things are very subjective, and we can never tell what a judge is looking for."

"You don't have to make me feel better, Ms. Liebling. I didn't do my best. I came to this city to be a violinist—to be great, not good. Now they're telling me I can't even win a conservatory competition."

"Joey, schatsy, when we had our little talk, I mentioned to you that it might be a good idea to take some time off. It has been very intense for you to live in the city and devote everything to your music for a semester. There are lots of things thirteen year old boys should be doing, and spending day and night with music is not necessarily one of them."

"But all the greats made it by working six to eight hours a day, not three, Ms. Liebling. How can I beat the competition without the hours?

"Joey, I can assure you that you have so much talent, you could do it in three hours. Look, Catherine and Gabriel do not spend more than three hours a day; I know this. Frankly, I heard you play today and, except for your first movement, which was . . . well, I don't know where you were while you were playing it . . . you blew all the competition away with your second and third movements. No one thought the other kids had a chance—even the judges weren't so sure, but they had to take your opening into consideration, and it was not focused. It was as if you suddenly 'girded your loins' and said, 'I'll show them what I've got, and I've got two movements left to do it.' "

"Is that true, Ms. Libeling? Were they really impressed?"

"Oh boy, I'll say. There is nothing robotic about you when you take that stage Joey. You give your audience everything that's in your soul. That's a rare thing, my dear. But you can't allow yourself to be uneven or unfocused for a minute in a competition, Joey. There will always be someone up there whose life depends on winning, and they will."

"I understood."

"There must be a balance, and maybe because kids like Catherine and Gabriel live in their own community, with their families, and have a place to run sometimes that's not a practice room, they can recharge better than you can this semester. If you go to your bedroom now, at your uncle's place, you're still in your practice room. You're surrounded day and night by the 'animal'—the music. You look out your window, you see Lincoln Center and all your aspirations."

"I thought all that being in the environment stuff

was supposed to help me focus."

"Sometimes, but every child is different. You know you were the favorite to win today, don't you?"

"Okay, is that supposed to make me feel better? So now I let down the school and the administration too?"

"No, Joey. You just forgot your purpose here for a few crucial weeks, that's all."

I couldn't think of anything to say.

"I think you'll find it again, schatsy. I know you will. Maybe think about moving back to Connecticut for the Fall. I'll give you longer lessons when you come in. That way, you won't be breathing the competition every day of your life. It's not healthy, you know."

I gave her a hug and said thanks. I could only think about facing my uncle now.

I walked home, trying the whole time to formulate what I was going to say to Uncle Mischa. I opened the door and Matti was washing the dishes.

"Hey, young one, how'd it go?"

"Not so well, Matti. I didn't win. I didn't even place."

"Oh, that's all right, Joey. Come here and have a cookie."

She seemed so earnest and the cookies smelled so welcoming.

"Look, I just baked them fresh for ya. We can still celebrate, hon. Let's celebrate that it's over. Let's celebrate that tomorrow is a new day, okay?"

"Yeah, but I can't believe I let my stupid fantasies get in the way of winning. What did I think? Was I ever going to be a 'normal' thirteen year old—going to parties, having time to do the things they all do on weekends? It's just not like that for me. If I want to be on top, I have to focus, and that means I have to be different."

"Well, thank goodness that yer in a place where lots of ye are different. Isn't that true, Joey?"

"Yeah, Matti, I guess we're just stuck with each other. I'd have to give up everything I am to be accepted at school, and there was a time when I thought I'd want to do that."

My uncle's studio door creaked open slowly.

"What's with the long faces in here? You didn't win, Joey?"

"Win? I didn't even get second place."

My uncle was silent. He walked over to the window and just stared . . . silently. I ate the cookie. It was comforting . . . the chocolate and soft dough. It brought me back to my childhood—the smells in my mom's kitchen, the gooeyness on the silver foil pan that was left over after she scraped each warm cookie off its bottom.

My uncle stayed at the window for about two minutes. That's a lot of silence—enough for me to fill with terrible thoughts. I didn't say anything, though. I was afraid to start something.

"It's only one competition," he whispered.

"What?" I asked, not sure I had heard correctly.

"I said it's only one competition. Figure out what went wrong and fix it for the next time. No one knew their piece better than you, and no one there could play it better than you. So figure out what happened and get past this."

"I couldn't concentrate, Uncle Mischa. I just couldn't focus."

"Yes, that happens sometimes. It's a learning process. Maybe I was too hard on you, you think?"

He turned toward me for the first time since he began speaking. He didn't really want me to answer that with a "yes."

"Look, you told me yourself that by thirteen, I should be able to take the harshest critiques in the world and put them in a professional perspective. Why would I want you to give me compliments if I didn't deserve them?"

Matti burst into the conversation boldly. I couldn't believe my ears.

"Yes, but a couple of 'good jobs,' and 'that's greats' would have been nice on occasion. It's way too 'adult'—how you are with that boy, Mischa. You're not like that with your other students."

"Matti, you shouldn't stick your nose into this. It's family business."

"Aye, and I'm part of the family. After all these years, Mischa, how do you suppose I see meself? And I'm telling ya, you expect way too much from him. He's a child. Not a professional."

"Please stop it! Both of you! I know what went wrong—I went wrong. Uncle Mischa was never too hard on me. I started wishing I was someone else, I became someone else, and I didn't like the way it felt." I put my hands over my face and bit my bottom lip hard . . . hard enough so I wouldn't even notice the wetness of tears pouring down my cheeks.

"So, do you know who you want to be now, Josef?"

I looked up at my Uncle. I didn't see the powerful artist I had created him into in my mind. I saw a hopeful but sad man who had devoted his life to the beauty of his craft. He didn't know how to separate my future from his past.

"Yes, Uncle Mischa," I stood and said out loud. "I know exactly who I want to be—Josef Cohen, the violinist. I'm going to be leaving for home when this semester finishes. I think I can remember all the wonderful things you taught me, and still live with my family away from Manhattan. It's not your fault either, so don't blame yourself. It's just something I guess I had to go through."

I knew he thought he had failed, but I didn't. My uncle didn't say a word. He walked back into his studio. There would be no practicing today.

CHAPTER 15

MISHAPS AT THE MUSIC INSTITUTE

Five weeks to go now before the end of conservatory in May. We had one more major struggle—four of us were entered by our teachers and administration to compete in the Junior Tchaikovsky Competition. It was a ridiculous premise anyway—that one of their young concert violinists could possibly win over one of the high school or college age violinists. It was, I have to say, intolerable pressure to put on kids our age. But as I told you all earlier, we were never treated our age. In this business you have no business being in it unless you plan to win it! Many of us had to miss school days just to finish learning our concertos.

Two weeks had now passed since the first competition. On Saturday Catherine and I got to orchestra early, as usual. Everyone slowly sifted in, until all the seats were filled—all except . . . where was Lavinia? This was now the second Saturday in a row she missed. At first we thought she was just sick last week, but Lavinia hadn't missed a Saturday in three years. She came whether she was sick, tired, sick and tired, or catching a plane the same afternoon. Orchestra began and ended and Lavinia never arrived. I kept looking over at Catherine to see if she had any idea what happened. "I mouthed the words, "Where's

Lavinia?"

She shrugged her shoulders and mouthed back, "Maybe she's got a gig."

Neither Catherine nor I would find out till later.

At the end of orchestra we asked Maestro Herrington if he knew what happened to Lavinia. He said he had heard different things, but if we were so interested, we should ask at the office.

There were fifteen minutes between orchestra class and our respective theory classes. We decided to check out the office. It was odd not seeing Lavinia's mother pacing around the lobby. That was one of the familiar sights on a Saturday afternoon at prep. We knocked on the office door, which was always open any way. The director of our conservatory, Dr. Meryl Marcus was inside. Catherine spoke first.

"Hi Dr. Marcus. Joey and I just came from orchestra and we were worried about Lavinia. She wasn't there this week or last and she hasn't missed a class in three years. Do you have any idea what happened?"

"Well, actually I do guys, but I'm not at liberty to talk about it. Lavinia won't be back next year. It was her decision though, her mother says."

Oh my, I thought to myself, *what did her mother do to her? They must have had a fight. Maybe Lavinia wasn't allowed to play anymore. Maybe Lavinia had a nervous breakdown from it all and decided to just quit. Maybe I should call her house.*

"Oh," said Catherine. "Okay, Dr. Marcus. We'll giver her a call."

"I don't know if you'll find her at home, guys."

"Why not?" Catherine's curiosity was peaked now.

"Well, you can try," is all Dr. Marcus would add.

"Oh, now this is a mystery," Catherine said.

"I'm going to call after classes, Cat. I'll come find you in the hall later."

"Yeah, please don't forget. I'll be dying to know."

"Okay. Later."

We both went to our theory classes. Then I had chamber. Finally I was free and made a mad dash for the public telephone. I had to call Lavinia's house.

"Hello. This is Joey. May I please speak to Lavinia?"

Lavinia's mother sounded like she had been crying. Her voice was very soft. She certainly didn't sound like she wanted to speak to me.

"Lavinia not here. Lavinia not here no more. Joey, I can't talk now."

"Wait. What do you mean? Did she run away or something?"

"What you mean, what I mean? How do you know about running away? Lavinia talk to you about this? You know her plan? Tell me Joey Cohen."

Ah, again with the Joey Cohen. That's where Lavinia got it from.

"No, no, I was just guessing. I mean, you said she's not here any more."

"Well, she no run away. She take plane and go back to China."

"China? For the summer? Cool."

"Not cool, nothing cool about it. Lavinia made plan with my mother to come live with her till she finish high school. She continue to study with her old teacher. The teacher say she teach her for no pay. Can you believe? No pay. So Lavinia tell us she take her savings and buy ticket to China and that's that. I

177

don't know why she do this thing. Do you know why? Did she tell you?"

"Uhhh, no, she never said a word about this. I'm as shocked as you are."

What was I gonna' say, after all? Oh, sure, as a matter of fact your daughter had a whole conversation with me about this a month ago, and she thinks you care more about her music than her? I don't think her mom would have liked to hear that.

"Well, now you know the whole story," she said.

None of us would ever know the whole story! They were dropping like flies. Valery runs off with a super model, Lavinia runs away to China. Who was next? I got off the phone and walked out of the hallway in a daze. I almost walked smack into Ms. Liebling.

"Schatsy, it's good I'm bumping into you. You won't believe what a wonderful opportunity I have for you."

That snapped me out of my daze. Some good news for a change.

"What, Ms. Liebling? I could use some good news right about now."

"Welllllll . . ." (Ms. Liebling always would do this "sing-song" thing with her words when she was happy.)

"I just spoke to one of the most famous violinists of our time. He's eighty-two years old now and, of course, doesn't concertize anymore, but you certainly will know his name when I tell you. Anyway, he is coming to A.I.M. next weekend and he would like to hear performances by the top two or three young concert violinists at our school. The committee selected you as one of them, Joey. You are going to play for the very great Sascha Berlinsky!"

There was silence. She was waiting for me to jump up and down and who knows what else, but I couldn't move. "Sascha Berlinsky? You mean The Sascha Berlinsky? The one my uncle Mischa played for forty-two years ago?" *I guess as you get older you get more adjectives attached to your name; when Grandma spoke of him he was only the "great" Berlinsky.*

Ms. Liebling paused, "Oh my goodness, Joey, I didn't even think of that. But your name is Cohen and his is Golub; Berlinsky won't make the connection."

"Yeah, but I will. I don't know if I can do it. I mean, play for the man who single-handedly ruined my uncle's career? Could you do it, Ms. Libeling?"

"Joey, listen to me. What happened to your uncle was definitely one of the cruelest things I've ever heard in the business; but it happened to your uncle—not to you. You are a new generation, Joey. And if you play your cards right, and move very intelligently, you will have the career your uncle never had. You mustn't let his past ruin your future."

"Wow, I really don't know what to say. I have to run it by Uncle Mischa. Can I tell you for sure tomorrow? I'll call you."

"All right, Joey, but you have to make this decision for yourself. Mischa is not going to be happy about you doing it, you know that."

"That's putting it mildly. I have to talk it over with him though, okay? Please don't be mad, Ms. Liebling."

"I'm not, Joey. I'm just concerned for you. I want you to make the right choices. Call me tomorrow, schatsy."

She walked back toward the elevator. Well, at least

she was still calling me "schatsy." I know it meant a lot to her for Berlinsky to hear me. I just wasn't yet sure what it meant to me.

Wait till I tell Catherine everything that transpired. What a day!

CHAPTER 16

THE FALL OF VUNDERFALL

I was on my way to Catherine's chamber music classroom on the first floor, near the elevator. I figured I'd get there before the rest of her quartet arrived. Suddenly, out of the usual buzzing in the hallway came the sounds of screams streaming out from Dupont Hall, the main auditorium where Maestro Vunderfall's orchestra met each morning.

Students were running down the hall calling to teachers and office workers to come quickly to the auditorium, and to call an ambulance. What happened? Did the maestro have a heart attack?"

Catherine ran over to one of the hysterical older students. "What happened? Did something happen to the maestro?"

"To the maestro? Certainly not. That maniac threw one of his Beethovenesque fits again, hurled a metal chair off the stage and this time, hit the little sister of our first cellist, Clara, right in the forehead. She's lying on the floor now with the corner of her forehead split open, bleeding and crying. We knew this would happen one day! The guy's a maniac."

"Oh my," shrieked Cat, "I can't believe he did that."

Personally, I couldn't believe one of Vunderfall's students had the guts to call him a maniac. We all knew he was, but he was such an amazing conductor, and inspired such respect, no one would dare say a word about his "little anger management problem."

"Joey, that could have been one of us in there. We're gonna' have him next year."

"Correction," I said, "you mean we were gonna' have him. This screams law suit, Cat."

"You think they'll fire him?"

"Of course, would you want your child in the orchestra with that guy? No mother here will stand for that."

"Oh My goodness! That poor little girl! Should we go see if we can help?"

"Honestly, I think they'd all appreciate it more if we stayed out of everyone's way. The police have to come, she'll have to go for stitches, the school has to calm down, classes have to resume. Nope, let's get to class. We'll check up on Clara later at the office, okay?"

"Okay, but I'm not gonna' be able to tell a whole note from an eighth note till I know what happens with the maestro."

We headed straight for the elevator. On the sixth floor, I got out and ran right into Noah.

"Did you hear what happened to Vunderfall?" Noah asked

"Yeah, but you weren't around, how did you hear?" I questioned.

"From Wu," he said.

"How did he hear?" I asked.

"From Chang," he added

"But who told him?" I asked.

"Chin—'cause his sister is in Vunderfall's viola section. Are you kidding, all of Manhattan knows by now." The school was reeling. This would be all over the papers, unless they could contain it. Schools are usually pretty good at keeping their demons behind closed doors, so I expected it would blow over.

I was going to tell Cat about the Berlinsky thing, but I didn't have the energy at this point. Too much going on. I had to just get to class and then home to speak to Uncle Mischa—man to man.

By five o'clock I was home, and Matti met me in the kitchen with a tall iced tea and a bowl of Tofu with Black Bean Sauce (one of my favorites). I was very quiet through dinner, until Uncle Mischa emerged from his studio.

"Hi, Uncle Mischa. Long day?"

"Oh, if I have to correct one other person's intonation today, I think I'll become an electrician. I'd learn on the job. Wires, violin strings . . . what's the difference. A string is a string, right?. What do you think, Joe?"

"I think you shouldn't quit your day job."

"So, what's doing at the conservatory these days?"

"Oh, you know, the usual. I had my scale class . . . it was good; I had orchestra . . . it was interminable . . . I had my lesson, and Ms. Liebling wants me to play for Berlinsky . . . I had my coaching with Professor Krantz and . . ."

"WHAT DID YOU SAY?"

"Uh, which part?"

"The part about . . . BERLINSKY!!!"

"Uh, Ms. Liebling said I was selected to perform for Berlinsky when he comes to the school on Saturday."

"He's coming? BERLINSKY is coming?"

You would have thought we were talking about the

Redcoats or something hugely historical.

"Yes, and he is going to hear me play. What do you think I should play for him?"

"What do I think you should play for him?"

"Uncle Mischa, do you realize you are just repeating my questions? Tell me what to play."

"JOSEF COHEN, YOU ARE NOT PLAYING FOR BERLINSKY! NOT NOW, NOT SATURDAY, NOT EVER."

"But Uncle Mischa."

"No buts. Are you out of your mind? The man ruined my career. He's a psycho!"

I have to admit, that did seem like a mildly funny statement coming from my uncle.

"I know, Uncle Mischa, but that was a long time ago. He's 82 years old now, and he can't hurt anyone. He's not concertizing anymore."

"But, how could you even think of reliving this for me? I couldn't let you go, Joey—out of principle."

The interesting thing about this conversation is that, when I started it, I wasn't at all sure of how I felt about playing, but now . . . I was positive.

"Look, your experience doesn't have to be mine. I won't even ask you to practice the piece with me this week. But I'm curious to know what he thinks of me. You're the one who told me I can do it, and that the city is listening and all that bunk!"

"It's not bunk. It's all true."

"So, I need a little success, Uncle Mischa, let me have it."

"But what if he cuts you down? Are you going to leave music? One word from Berlinsky can be like poison."

"But his words to you, initially, were wonderful."

"Who knows what he really thought. Maybe he was being kind at the moment. Maybe he was afraid to have his name linked with mine because he thought I wasn't great enough. How do I know what was on this man's mind?"

"I don't know how to answer that, Uncle Mischa, but I'm going under my own name and my own steam. I have to know, can't you understand that?"

"You do this, Josef . . . you do it alone. You fail, you fail alone. You succeed, then . . . good for you. But don't expect me to support you in this."

It was hard to swallow the words Uncle Mischa had for me, but this was a path I had to follow. I practiced like a demon for the next six days. On the seventh day, I met Berlinsky

I didn't go to any of my classes that Saturday. I slept late, practiced for two hours and walked to A.I.M. I felt tremendously strong for some reason. Maybe some of that was the large, shiny chip I had on my shoulder. I was going to show him he couldn't keep my family down. He pushed one down, and another one popped up! I knew I couldn't tell him who I was. I was just going for his comments and years of expertise.

I knocked on Ms. Liebling's door. She opened it with a big smile.

"Ah, Maestro Berlinsky, this is my little Joey. Wait till you hear him."

Oh boy, I had to actually shake hands with this man. I hadn't thought that one through.

"Well, young man, a fine looking young man you are. Let's hear you play, my boy."

I took a good, long look at him. He was a small man, slight in build with very straight, defined shoulders, probably from years of great violin posture. His face was slightly wizened but with very young eyes that sparkled and teased. They had lived a life of great pleasure; seen many successes and many important people. They were happy eyes. They didn't look like the eyes of a "destroyer."

"It's a great honor to meet you. I've grown up listening to your recordings."

"Ah, those scratchy, old things. There were only two I really liked," he teased. "Why don't you show me how it's done now?

This was it. I would play for Berlinsky, and he didn't even know who I was. I took my place in front of the bend in the piano, nodded to the accompanist and played. What did I play? The third movement of the *Brahms Violin Concerto*. Would he remember? Hundreds of young hopefuls had probably played that specific movement of that specific piece for him. But no one had a better reason for playing it. My uncle had taught it to me, phrase by phrase, with remarkable love and patience and detail. I began.

As I played I was very conscious of every expression and dynamic. I had to make every phrase purposeful. I had to keep total focus; to go deep inside. I had to because, as Ms. Liebling once put it, my life depended on it.

The final chords. I was actually sweating. I turned slowly toward the man. He looked at me with great seriousness, then exploded in applause. He stood up.

"Well . . ." pause . . . "That was remarkable . . . truly. . . . I mean . . . how old are you?"

"Thirteen," I said.

"Thirteen? What a soul! It has been a very long time since someone your age played the Brahms for me . . . a very long time."

I had done it. He loved it . . . I had to tell him. Oh, I was bursting. He couldn't do anything to me, because I would never use his name. The experience would be mine—only mine. I had to let him know.

"Was it Mischa Golub?" I asked.

"What? " He asked cautiously and slowly.

"Mischa Golub? Was that the last 13 year old who played the Brahms for you?"

"Well, yes. I think it was. I don't usually hear too many youngsters who can pull that off. How do you know about that?"

"I'm his nephew," I said proudly, but without any anger.

No one spoke. Berlinsky looked at my teacher. She kept her head down, as if to say, "Oh no, here we go again." He looked back at me.

"You know, I thought I noticed you using some of the same creative fingerings Golub used to do. They were unusual. Most teachers wouldn't pick them, but he was known for unusual fingerings. Somehow, I understand, he made them work. He was very great, your uncle. Does he coach you?"

"Yes sir, he works with me a great deal."

"Good, good. No wonder. You have his passion and his left hand. He was the greatest young prodigy I had ever heard, you know." He shook his head knowingly.

"Was he?" I asked proudly.

"Oh, without question. A shame what happened." There was an awkward silence. I did nothing to fill it.

187

"Anyway, you have it too. You will work very hard and become very great, won't you? You're in the right hands with Ms. Liebling, just don't let your uncle sour you to this. Your talent is too big. You will one day make the name he couldn't."

I was about to explode. I wanted to "let him have it." What did he mean, "It's a shame what happened to him?" He was what happened to him. I had to watch myself. Couldn't step over the line.

"Well, thank you so much for hearing me. I'll never forget this." I shook his hand strongly and stood straight and confidently.

"Good boy," he said, "no hint of a 'bow.' You'll go far. Goodbye Josef Cohen, nephew of Mischa Golub."

I gave Ms. Liebling a hug and left. The door closed. I took a deep breath and looked out toward the elevators. "Berlinsky approved," I whispered. I pressed "down."

When I first arrived home, Mischa didn't come out of his studio. I waited for an hour, just sitting in the living room, reading. Finally the door opened slowly.

"Well, I see you're here."

"You know I've been here for an hour, Uncle."

"So?"

"So, what do you want to know first? How I did, or what he thought of you?"

"He told you what he thought of me?"

"He certainly did."

"You told him who you were?"

"I certainly did."

"What did he think of you, Josef? Tell me what he said."

"He stood up for me."

"He stood? Berlinsky stood for you?"

"He said that it was remarkable."

"*The Bruch*?"

"Nope, the *Brahms.*"

"You played the *BRAHMS VIOLIN CONCERTO* for BERLINSKY?" He roared.

"Only the last movement. Look, I knew he'd like it, because you taught it to me, and we all know what he thought of you."

"You played the *Brahms* for Berlinsky, 42 years after I did? There's something very mystical about that."

"Uncle Mischa, he said I will have a very great career. He recognized some of your fingerings. You see what an impression you made?"

"I can't hear any more. . . . What did he look like?"

"He looked good—nice, not monstrous—but the years might have softened him. Anyway, don't you want to know what he said about you?"

My uncle turned toward the window. "I can't hear any more."

"He said you were the greatest young violinist he had ever heard." I left out the part about it being a shame that Mischa never made it. I didn't think he'd appreciate it.

"He said that? You didn't prompt him or any-thing?"

Look at this, a man of 55 years, reduced to a young hopeful just at the mention of a compliment from this musical icon. There was something very sad about that to me.

"No, I didn't prompt. He meant it. So you see, now you've succeeded and I've succeeded."

"What do you mean?"

"You know what he had always thought about you, and I now know that if I could play for Berlinsky and succeed, I can do anything."

Mischa turned around, walked slowly across the rug, and enfolded me in one of his big, uncle bear hugs. "I told you, Joey, the city is listening."

It took about two weeks for American Institute to return to business as usual. Things did eventually calm down a bit since Vunderfall's fall from grace and Lavinia's disappearance. We all settled into our classes and tried to act "normal." The only odd thing I did notice was that Gabe had been absent for the past two weeks. Now, this was possible, I guess, if someone had two big orchestral concerts in a row, or if someone was deathly sick, but neither rang true. First of all, two weeks was an awfully long time to be sick, secondly, if he had such big concerts, we'd all know about it—orchestral gigs don't stay a secret in our school, and thirdly, you just don't stay out two weeks in a row in our kind of program, because you won't remain in the program.

When I saw Catherine in orchestra I asked her opinion. "I don't mean to be paranoid or anything, but did you notice Gabe hasn't been here for two weeks?"

"Notice? I've been positively miserable about it."

"Well, doesn't that strike you as odd?"

"What? Being miserable?"

"No, no, no . . . his not being here either."

I don't know. Two in a row is a bit much. I would know if he had big concerts. He would have told me—at least I think he would've. Who knows with him?

Hmmm . . . did I detect a morsel of disgust with this Gabe scenario?

"Exactly," I added innocently.

"So what are you saying? He didn't run off to China with Lavinia!" laughed Catherine.

"No, but I bet ya he's not back next Saturday. I just have this feeling."

"So melodramatic! Okay. I'll be sure to check in with you next week, detective, to see how your hypothesis shapes up."

No more talking. It was time for the downbeat.

CHAPTER 17

VANISHING VIOLINISTS

The following Saturday came and this time, not only was there no Gabe, but there was also no Noah in scale class. I couldn't wait to see Catherine in orchestra. I didn't have to wait too long, because just as I was finishing my scale there was a knock on the practice room door. It was Cat.

"Cat, what's up?"

"He's not here. You were right. And neither is Noah. I saw Noah's mom, Gabe's mom and Lavinia's mom in the office this morning."

"Oh . . . my. . . . What did they say is going on?"

"I don't know exactly, but what's worse is a note I found in my mail slot," Catherine said agitatedly.

All the advanced students at American Institute had their own mail slots so conductors and directors of various festivals and musical venues could leave messages for them easily.

"What kind of note?"

"Come out here and read it. And you better sit down, Joey."

I told my scale teacher I was leaving, packed up my fiddle and went out into the hall. I sat down on the worn carpeting with my knees bent up in front of me. "Okay, I'm ready. Lay it on me!"

Catherine handed me a note, frayed at the edges, like someone had taken a match to it. It had letters pasted together on it from newspaper print. It read:

"Thought you could beat me, but you'll never know
  The exposition's unraveling—how far will I go?
  Curious? Meet me on top of the third,
  at 6:00 P.M., music like you've never heard."

"What is this?" I gasped. "Is someone trying to spook you?"

"I don't know, Joey, but get this—all three of the other kids who've disappeared received similar notes in their mail slots before their disappearance."

"Where did you find this? And how do you know all this?" I sputtered.

"I told you, it was in my mail slot this morning. I pretended I was hanging out reading my mail so I could hear what the mothers and the director were talking about. It seems that the director's assistant had mentioned seeing the same odd looking, burnt notes in Noah, Gabe, and Lavinia's slots over the past few weeks. And now they're gone!."

"Lavinia had one too? I thought her mom said she'd left for China?"

"Yes, but her mom never actually saw her go. She has just received postcards from her—or, at least, ostensibly from her."

"So did you go to the director and tell her you got one too?" I asked nervously.

"No, I wanna' go and check it out—with you. We can do it together. Whoever it is won't be expecting two of us, right? We'll fake him out. Safety in numbers and all that stuff!"

"Cat, no offense, but you're out of your mind. Gabe is missing, Lavinia and Noah, all in a few weeks, now you have some creepy letter that they all received and which probably led to their kidnapping, and you want to go the same route? You've been doing toooo much practicing—your poor little brain has obviously collapsed under the pressure. Let me make this simple for you ... NOOOOOOO!"

Oh please Joey, please. Where's your spirit of adventure? We could nail this case."

I couldn't believe my ears.

"What case? There is no case? The only 'case' here is you! You could be walking right into the hands of a murderer here and you don't care? Go tell the director. That's my final offer!" *Ah, the voice of reason, or was it the voice of chicken? I couldn't tell, but it was pretty loud! All I knew is we shouldn't do it.*

Catherine looked so sad. You'd think I had just turned her down for the prom or something. "Look Cat, I'd do anything for you, but I'm not risking both our lives."

"Oh poo. If you're gonna be a stick in the mud, I'll do it myself." She turned and stormed down the hall.

I was not a happy camper! But when I said no, I meant NO!!!

Ten minutes later I was following Cat up the stairs to the third floor. . . . I'm so decisive.

We reached the top of the stairs.

"See, nothin' up here. Let's go," I said quickly.

"Yeah, but I want to see where he might hide later. And where his escape route might be?"

"Why? So you can jump out from the elevator and

go 'Peak A Boo'???"

"No, Joey, come on, take this seriously."

"I'm the only one here taking this seriously."

I watched as Catherine sniffed out all the alcoves. I couldn't believe she expected to return here at 6:00 P.M. as prescribed by the kidnapper. I didn't know what to say to stop her. Luckily our next class was in five minutes.

"Look, we've got to go. I'll meet you in the lobby at 5:45, when the school is clearing out, and we'll talk about it again, okay."

"Ah, my hero!" Catherine was quite pleased with her persuasive abilities.

"Yeah, yeah, save it! I'll see ya later."

We parted company. I had to do something drastic within the next few hours—and that did not include going to class!

CHAPTER 18

MYSTICAL DIVERSION

Back at the apartment, my uncle was spending some quality time with his "Kabbalah." What I mean is that he spent the morning in his studio studying the Zohar, which he did every Saturday morning. He loved his time alone with the mystical writings of Judaism. I never fully understood what he was learning or why Matti and I would hear the sounds of breaking glass coming from there during his study, but, to tell you the truth, I was always afraid to ask. He had only explained to me that he studied Kabbalah to get further meaning into life, and become more connected with His Creator.

You see, the Hebrew word Kabbalah means "received tradition." It represents the vast study of Jewish mysticism, with its origins in *Sefer Ha-Zohar* (*The Book of Splendor*) from the 13th century. Those who study it believe it to be the key to the mystical union of the physical world with the spiritual world; the union of God—the Creator, with that which was created (i.e.—us). The *Zohar* is the most important among the Kabbalistic works. It is said to have been written between 1280 and 1286 in Spain. It deals with the ten sefirot (spheres) emanating from the Infinite (God), which is called Ein Sof. Through these spheres and Ein Sof, the universe is, supposedly, maintained. The concepts behind Kabbalah are very intense, and way too mature for a thirteen year old, but I'm doing my best here!

So, the idea is that Ein Sof (God, the Infinite) contracts at the beginning of creation to allow room for cosmic expansion. During this contraction, the spheres (sefirot) explode, shatter and fall to, what became earth. Therefore, redemption, or wholeness (putting the sefirot back together) is what humans are searching to do throughout their lives. We are looking for the pieces of the divine in ourselves and trying to repair the world and make it whole. Each one of us must find his own path to wholeness in order to find God and this spark of good and happiness in us. So, repairing the world (tikkun olam), becomes the overriding thrust of our existence. Heavy, huh?

So that's what my uncle was up to as I walked in the door, six hours early from conservatory. I turned the key and didn't hear Matti's usual melodious humming. That was odd. I shut the door and began walking toward Mischa's studio. He came flying out in a flash, looking very disoriented, carrying his copy of the Tchaikovsky orchestra score under his arm.

"What are you doing home so early, Joey? Is everything all right?" He asked nervously.

"Uh, sure, sort of." I was about to tell him the bizarre tale when a slip of paper came floating out of his score and onto the floor. He didn't notice it because he was already walking toward the sofa. I bent down and picked it up, fully intending to return it to my uncle, but there . . . staring me in the face . . . were four names in block letter print: LAVINIA,

GABRIEL, NOAH, CATHERINE.

I took a deep gulp and shoved the paper into my pocket. How did Mischa know these students were missing? And if he didn't know, why were their names specifically printed on one piece of paper?

"So?"

"Uh, so what?" I asked, as if being awakened from a reverie.

"So why are you here so early?"

Now what would I say? How could I tell my uncle about the kidnappings at the institute if my uncle might be the one who's doing the kidnapping?

"Well, my next period teacher was sick and I thought I'd grab lunch at home for a change and surprise you." *That was pretty good,* I thought. *Keep calm. It's just a regular day . . . get up, go to music school, see friends, find out your uncle's a kidnapper...*

"Oh, well, that's a very nice surprise. I'm sorry I gave Matti the day off to attend a matinee with her friend, otherwise I'd have her prepare lunch for you. But you can find something, I'm sure. I just have a little work to finish up in my study and I'll join you."

Yeah, I bet he had work to do!. "Okay, Uncle Mischa. I'll make myself a sandwich."

He disappeared seamlessly into the studio, and I gathered some clothes. As I was leaving, I heard him dialing the phone. I picked up the receiver in the living room.

"A.I.M., good morning. How may I address your call?"

"I am calling to tell you that you must . . . you must close your school early today. There is another kidnapping planned. You must close before 5:00 P.M."

"Wait, sir . . . who is going to be kidnapped? How do you know?" The administration was alarmed, not just about his call, but that he had said "another" kidnapping, intimating that he knew there had been others already. This information had not leaked to the public as far as they knew.

"That's all. Please do as I say."

"No, don't hang up. Please wait . . ." The phone line was dead. My uncle had done his job. He knew if he stayed on too long his call could be traced.

I tore out of the apartment and headed for A.I.M.

A frenzy ensued at American Institute of Music. Everyone in the office was huddled together, trying to figure out how to close the school without creating a panic. They decided on a fire drill that would result in complications, requiring the students to stay off the premises. They would tell the kids that on one floor the emergency sprinkler system had been activated (during the drill), and could not be fixed that afternoon. So, all students were asked to please contact their parents and make arrangements for early dismissal.

I found Catherine at the far end of the school with her fiddle and notebooks in hand, pacing like an expectant father.

"Cat, listen, can I come stay at your house tonight? I can't stay with my uncle. Something terrible's come up. I'll tell you all about it, but we have to be away from here."

"Sure Joey, that's fine. But what's up? He's not sick is he?"

"No, let's talk as we walk."

We ran across the street and half way down the

block before I began explaining. I turned around twice to make sure no one from the school was behind us, then I spilled the beans.

"Cat, I know who is doing the kidnapping."

"Get outta' here. What are you talking about?"

"My uncle. I know it's him. I caught him. I couldn't believe it, but the evidence was overwhelming."

"Overwhelming evidence? What did you find, a bunch of bodies tied up under his piano or something? No, let me guess, you heard wild strains of chamber music coming from his studio in the middle of the night, and you know he can only play one instrument at a time!" Catherine was laughing uncontrollably. She was sure I had gone off the deep edge.

"No Cat, get serious."

"You get serious! We're talking about your uncle here—Mischa Golub—a legend in the music world. You had better have pretty persuasive evidence, Joey, before you go around accusing Mischa Golub."

"Listen to me. A piece of paper slipped out from one of his orchestral scores. It had the names of all our friends who were kidnapped: Lavinia, Gabe, Noah, and then you, Cat. It had your name on it. What was he doing with such a list? How did he know what had happened at the school? I never told him. The story had been hushed within the school until they had more evidence. I only knew because you overheard the director talking to those mothers in her office. Why did he have that list, Cat?"

"I have to admit that is creepy."

"I know. And what is he doing all the time in that study of his? I've never been in there you know. Neither has Matti. In fact, Matti wasn't there today.

Maybe she's gone now too."

"No, don't be silly. She's worked for him for years."

"I don't know what to think anymore. Why would he do such a thing?"

"I can't really answer that, Joey. He has had an infamously disappointing life, though. He must be bitter. He's definitely eccentric, right? Everyone says he is. Maybe all his life's disappointments have been welling up inside him and he finally cracked. You know, imploded!"

"You mean maybe he couldn't take it anymore that young kids were being recognized as great artists and his chance was taken from him at the height of his prodigy? Maybe he's doing this to get revenge?"

"That's a scary thought. . . . But your uncle teaches great young violinists. I know a bunch of kids that would kill to get into his teaching studio, but he had no room for them. He molds his students—nurtures them. Does it make sense to you that he'd stoop to such a thing?"

Ultimately I had no answer for that. Within minutes we were in front of Catherine's building. There was a rumbling of thunder in the distance, then a momentary bolt of lightening—unannounced, menacing. It was close to us. The rain could not be far behind. We ducked into the lobby.

Catherine told her mom that my uncle wasn't well, and asked if it would be all right if I stayed with them a couple of nights. Thankfully she loved me, so she said yes. She left to pick up some extra groceries. We completed all our homework for school and tried not to think about the A.I.M. caper! It was now 6:00 P.M.—the time Cat was supposed to meet the unidentified author of the note. I watched the hands of the clock move haltingly past 6:10, 6:15, and 6:20. At 6:30 P.M. there was a knock at the door.

"Catherine, Joey, are you there? It's Uncle Mischa. Please let me in."

Catherine and I were temporarily paralyzed. We stood like stone figures in the living room, petrified and laden with the burden of truth. I opened the door.

"Uncle Mischa, how did you know where I was?"

"Well, you weren't home by 3:30 or 4:00 or 5:00. You didn't say any classes were running later today, and the person you're closest to is Catherine. So I had to go with that. I was worried about you. These are uncertain times, my boy."

"I'm sorry," Joey conceded.

"You never did this before. Why didn't you call?"

"Well, uh," I looked to Catherine for support. "The school was closed suddenly and Cat and I figured we'd, uh . . . no that's not the whole story. Uncle Mischa, do you know what's been going on at A.I.M?"

"Yes, Joey, I've heard."

"Well, how did you hear? I never said anything."

"If I told you, you wouldn't understand," Uncle Mischa replied, his eyes sweeping the floor in embarrassment."

At this point I was physically trembling. I had to tell Uncle Mischa about finding that slip of paper. "Uncle, I found a piece of paper that was tucked into your Tchaikovsky score. It had all the names of the kids from American Institute who were recently kidnapped. They had received notes, frayed at the edges by fire, instructing them to meet some stranger somewhere in the school at some predetermined time. All we know after that is the kids disappeared. Would you know anything about this?"

Mischa knew now that I suspected him. He had to regain my trust. "Yes, Joey, I know about it. But no, I had nothing to do with it," he insisted.

"Joey, what I'm going to tell you may sound impossible, but you must believe it is the truth. You know I have studied the Kabbalah for many years and have very advanced understanding of the human connection with the Infinite."

Oh, here we go, I thought. I had little patience for this stuff. I could barely understand New York, how was I supposed to understand the cosmos?

"The voices I hear when I study, you know, the inspirations I get, they guide me through the mysteries of life. They have been a great comfort to me through the disappointments of my youth. You must understand, the Kabbalah, like the Bible is a very noisy document."

By this point Cat and I were staring at each other and freaking out. He hears voices? A noisy document? My uncle is delusional. That's it. He's lost his marbles! A little too much Tchaikovsky, no doubt! These "voices of the masters" must be telling him to go and kidnap little prodigies and put them out of their misery. Holy smoke! How would I ever tell Grandma that her son had snapped? I motioned to Catherine with my eyes to get inside the bedroom and call the police. She excused herself for a moment and shut the bedroom door behind her. Uncle Mischa kept talking. I never knew he had so much to say. He never spoke to me unless it was about music. He never told me his heart.

"What I mean by noisy, Joey, is that the Kabbalah

carries within its pages the voices of the masters from years ago, and all their commentary. It is full of voices, Joey, just like the pages of your music.

I had truly never thought of music that way before, and I had to admit it made some sense.

"So when I come to study it, I bring my voice to its text as well. But as I've gotten older, my life's frustrations, anger and disappointments have begun to clog the purity of my mind. I have not been able to come to the text with clean, happy, open pathways. Each time I try to study, the anger inside me shatters the glass of the spheres all over again. It's like the world must be recreated for me anew each time I try to find wholeness through the words of the masters."

Oh my, the shattering sounds Matti and I would hear so often—it was the reenactment of the spheres of the world breaking apart to form our world. Because my uncle was such a deeply spiritual and perceptive individual, and such a scholar on top of that, he would enliven, on a small scale, through the shattering of a glass, a reenactment of the universal shattering. My uncle could never achieve peace and wholeness because he carried such destructive baggage—such sadness and bitterness. He couldn't let go. He was constantly reshattering the "glass." I got it now.

"You look as if you understand me. Do you, Joey?"

"I'm trying, Uncle."

"Well, today, as I was studying I had a powerful inspiration that came as if to give me a second chance in life. The voices in my mind told me about the terrible kidnappings going on at your school. I somehow heard the names of the victims. They told me I had a chance to make it all right again—to become whole. So I called your school and told them to close down, before it was too late—before they lost another one."

"So you were the reason we closed early today?" I was in disbelief. I needed to sit. I offered my uncle a drink.

Meanwhile, back in Catherine's room, she was having an animated discussion with Manhattan's finest! The door was left ajar and I could hear parts of her very unusual conversation with "the law."

"No, I don't know for sure and I have no evidence, but my friend and I have a hunch that the kidnapper himself is sitting in my living room right now. What?.. . . . What is he doing? Well, I don't know, I'll take a look, hold on . . ."

Catherine peeked out through the opening in her door. "Um, it appears that they're having drinks . . . yes, the kidnapper and my friend are having sodas in the living room . . . what? Well, yes, I'm aware of how that sounds. . . . No sir, I'm not playing Nancy Drew, and I do not have an overactive imagination, I'm telling you . . . where's my mother? She's at the super-market, what does that have to do with anything?" CLICK.

So much for a citizen's arrest. Catherine opened her door wider but stayed inside her room. She motioned for me to come toward the door. I excused myself from my uncle momentarily.

"What is it? I'm in the middle of a heavy discussion with my uncle. I don't think he did it anymore, at least I'm not as sure as I was an hour ago."

"Oh, that's just great. I make a fool of myself with the neighborhood police and now you say he's not the kidnapper."

"Look, Catherine, this whole thing is way too strange for me to make heads or tails out of. We have to wait it out. He seems so sincere though."

"Oh fine. Then next Saturday you have to come with me if I get another one of these spooky letters, you hear me?"

"Okay, okay. Maybe Uncle Mischa will help us too. But I'm telling you, Cat, you owe it to the school to tell them about your letter. They have to get the police on it."

"Yeah, well, maybe we'll find him first," She was becoming a little too happy and cocky again.

"Yeah, sure, maybe" I said.

I decided to return home with my uncle and ask him to be available if we needed him next Saturday.

CHAPTER 19

THE MISTAKE

You know how they say that a guilty person always winds up making a mistake somewhere along the line? Well, Cat and I were waiting for that—waiting for him to trip up. Walking into American Institute this Saturday was like walking into Desert Storm! There were police all over the lobby, army guys outside the front doors. It seemed as though my uncle's call to them was just the thing to make the kidnappings a reality. Someone who knew something had actually gotten in touch from the "outside." There was a definite connection now between the conservatory and the missing kids. The police put a tap on the phone to trace all incoming calls. If Uncle Mischa called again he'd be held on suspicion. If we were to save any lives or get to the bottom of this, we'd have to do it quickly. I waited in the lobby by the mailboxes till Cat arrived.

"Well?" I asked.

"Well yourself. What?"

"Go check your mailbox already!"

Catherine fumbled through the detritus of the week and suddenly pulled out another letter. It was different. No burnt edges, no newspaper printed letters. The text was made up of script letters that had been pasted together from some magazine. Now that was unusual. There aren't too many magazines that print their articles in script. We had a lead.

"What does it say? Is there a poem?" I asked.

"You bet. It's weird. It says:

Almost ruined, this tryst of ours,
Your career almost made, you so want to be a star,
Come little one and meet the baton
That invites your debut, so your name may live on!
Tonight at 8:00, an important run through,
Bring your fiddle—but no one else with you.
We'll meet with the rest in the tower never entered,
Take the stairs to floor seven,
the secret door—left centered."

"Whoa, that's the letter all right. No doubt about it," I said with a bit of disbelief. I did think that perhaps this mystery person would lay off a week because the heat was being turned up with the police presence. But no, this was a desperate character.

"And it's signed this time, Joey. It says: 'Respectfully, The star maker.'"

"Cat, let's go to the cafeteria and figure out our next move." Catherine was now in total shock.

We walked downstairs in a daze.

"Who would call themselves a star maker?" she asked.

"Well, there have been great teachers who have been known that way. Look at Dorothy Delay. The media always called her that."

"Well, it can't be her, she's dead." Cat added wryly.

"Very funny."

"Your uncle could be seen that way, even though he doesn't make any introductions for anyone. His students always rise to the greatest heights in the business. What do ya think?"

"I've gotta' tell you, as sure as I was before about him, I'm just as unsure now. I really don't think he has it in him. He recognizes his bitterness and past disappointments. He's a scholar, he's trying to deal with them in a healthy way."

"You call hearing voices coming out of ancient tomes dealing in a healthy way?" Catherine asked incredulously.

She didn't understand what it was like to be deeply involved in anything religious. Her family was third generation American. No mysteries of the deep there!

"I'm just saying we have to leave our options open. We have to think of everyone as a suspect."

"Except us." She was beginning to get nervous now.

"Right, except us. Now, you know who we didn't think of? Who else might be called a star maker? Examine the words in your letter."

She reread the note quickly, stopping on the word "baton."

"Oh my, Joey . . . baton . . . a conductor—Maestro Vunderfall! He certainly has a bone to pick with the school!"

"Yeah, true, but why would he put kids' lives at risk? He's not that type is he?"

"He was as crazy as he was great, though. And besides, we don't know that he has put anyone at risk. He's just made them disappear, right?"

"True, but the terrible upset it has caused the school and the parents of these kids," I added.

"Well, that could be it. The parents were, ultimately, the ones who insisted on his being fired. They were afraid he'd injure another student. He might want to take revenge on them."

This was just too tidy a theory for me. They would look at him eventually because of that possible motive and he'd know that.

"It's too easy, Cat. It can't be the maestro."

"Okay, maybe it's someone who wants us to think it's the maestro."

"Well, it has disdain in those few lines, doesn't it? You know, "you so want to be a star."

"Yeah, you're right. Maybe it's someone who is really jealous of all of us, and wants to level the playing field."

"That's an interesting point, but who? What kind of person? A teacher, performer, another student?"

"A parent?" Catherine added—and stopped suddenly. "Joey, you don't think it's a parent, do you?"

"That would just be too sick." I said, but I did promise to keep an open mind.

As I was speaking I noticed Catherine peering over at a magazine some woman was reading at the next table.

"Joey," she whispered, "that woman is reading a magazine with script writing in it. All the text is in a script font. I've gotta get a hold of that."

"So go ask her if you could have it when she's finished."

Catherine sauntered over casually and asked, "Uh, hi, excuse me, but I wondered if I could just see that magazine for a minute . . . my mom has been looking for it on the newsstands." *Catherine was so cool.*

"Oh, of course, honey," the lady responded. "You can have it now, I'm done with it. I just found it lying on the table here."

"Thanks," said Catherine.

"Tell your mom you can find them at our corner newsstand on Broadway, down the block from the school."

"Thanks, I'll be sure to tell her."

Catherine took a flying leap back to our table and opened to the page that woman had been reading. It was true that the whole font of the magazine was in script; that was unusual. It was *Travel Magazine* containing beautiful photos and sophisticated articles. Catherine flipped through the pages of the articles, then suddenly . . .

"Oh my, Joey."

"What, what?"

"Look at the bottom of this page."

"There is no bottom, it's missing."

"Exactly, it's been cut out. A whole section has been cut out. Can you believe it. I found it. I know I found the source of the letter."

"Well, don't run away with yourself, take out the letter and see if the font matches exactly. The eye can play tricks on you, you know."

Catherine reached into her pocket and pulled out the note. She stared at it in disbelief.

"I have to find out who left this magazine here." She flipped it over, there was no subscription name on the back.

"Listen, that woman said you can find these at the

corner newsstand. Come with me, let's see if the owner of the stand remembers anybody fishy!"

"Oh, you think he's just gonna' offer up some shady characters to you—'Yes, little girl, there was a very fishy character who came by to purchase this magazine this morning! He wore three pairs of sunglasses, two pairs of pants, and it looked like he didn't want to be recognized.' "

"Very funny, Okay you're a very funny guy, we've established that. Now come with me."

We still had twenty minutes before our first class, so off we went. I have to admit the suspense was killing me. We reached the corner and asked the owner if he remembered who had purchased the travel magazine this morning. We knew it was a long shot.

"Actually," he said, "I only remember because they're regulars. It was Maestro Vunderfall, your director and the mom of that cute little Asian girl, Lavinia. I haven't seen the little girl around lately, though. Is she still in school?"

"Um, she's on a brief vacation," I said. I couldn't believe one of our suspects actually bought the magazine. Maybe he was thinking of taking a trip.

"You see, I knew Vunderfall was involved in this," Catherine blurted.

"Yeah, there certainly is mounting evidence, but I've got a question for you. What is Lavinia's mother doing here on a Saturday morning buying a magazine from the neighborhood newsstand? They live in New Jersey."

"Well, maybe she has business to take care of in the office," offered Catherine.

"But the office was empty this morning except for

police. And what could she possibly have to do in the office a month after her daughter has left the country?" I was suddenly very interested in Lavinia's mother.

The two of us mulled this over till we re-entered the building. As we entered the lobby, sure enough there was Lavinia's mother racing through the pews of cellos and basses lining the hallway leading to the side entrance. I called to her.

"Mrs. Chen, hi. How've you been?"

Lavinia's mom froze for a moment and peered over the sea of instruments toward the voice that pierced her cover.

"Ah, Joey, Catherine, how are you both? It has been long time."

"Yes," I answered carefully. "We didn't think we'd see you around here again."

"Well, I had some billing issues to take care of today."

Hmm, that seemed innocuous enough.

"How's Lavinia? Have you heard from her?" I asked.

"She writes to me that she's doing beautifully. Happy away from here. I don't know how she sounds, of course. I only get post cards."

Her eyes lighted momentarily on Catherine and the magazine she was holding. "Catherine, you planning a trip, too?" She laughed.

Catherine was stunned for a moment, but then realized she was holding the magazine face up with the title, *Travel*, in clean sight. "Ah, no, I just borrowed this from someone here. I was bored."

Catherine searched Mrs. Chen's face for some

flash of guilt or worry that she had that magazine, but none was apparent.

"Yes, my husband and I like that magazine very much. It always has interesting articles about places to go in Spain and China. Well, it was nice seeing you guys again," and she dashed off.

"Okay, that's it. This is getting too weird. I'm going to the director with my note. I'm not heading up to that tower without heavy artillery behind me," Catherine announced in all seriousness.

"What's in that tower, anyway? I never see anyone go up there," I queried.

"As far as I know that's where they keep the old orchestral scores with the notations on them from the great conductors of 50 to 75 years ago . . . you know, when they came to conduct the oldest student orchestras at A.I.M. The school never throws them out because the scores have become too valuable with the maestros' remarks scribbled all over them. So, they've laminated them all, put them in boxes, and placed them up in the tower. It's locked."

"So are they planning on making a museum in the school someday to show these off, or they're just keeping them in boxes?"

"No, they plan on renovating soon and making a gallery to hang important autographed photos and scores. It's a good idea, but I don't know anyone who has ever been up there. It's gotta' be creepy."

"Yeah, you go tell the director. You should have done that to begin with. I'm going to class and try to forget about all this. Let the police handle it from here."

We agreed on this being the plan of action.

"You know, Joey, it doesn't really mean everything to me to be famous, like the note makes it sound. I wouldn't sell my soul for it or anything," Catherine said suddenly.

"I know, Cat. But we do get awfully caught up in it all. I used to think school was my world, and thought about it all the time. Sure, I'd put in my three hours every day on fiddle, but I never felt it taking over my life. I didn't live for it—even with all the wonderful things that happened to me last year."

"Yeah, I'd kill for that—oops!" Catherine interjected. "I didn't mean it that way."

"I know, I know."

"So has that changed since you've gotten to Manhattan?"

"Sure has—definitely since I've gotten here, and since I've met my uncle and the kids here who are also at the top of their game. Now I live from Saturday to Saturday. I believe I could be one of the best. Like it's actually expected of me. It defines me now."

"That's Okay," Catherine interrupted. "I'm defined by my violin, too. I think that kind of thinking makes me a more serious contender."

"Yeah, but we're not in a prize-fighting ring. We're making music. It's awful pressure."

"Joey Cohen, you're such an idealist. If you're going to dabble in music you shouldn't be here. To be serious about anything there must be pressure and there must be competition. There are kids studying daily many more hours than we do. That's giving up your life. So what are you complaining about? Celebrity has come to you fairly easily so far. Now you just have to keep it up. And you didn't even have to hurt anybody to get where you are."

I listened with due respect. I just didn't want to become like Uncle Mischa or Vunderfall or Valery— who put everything they were into this music thing, only to discover later that it hadn't been worth it." Catherine went off to see our director. I went off to class. 8:00 P.M. loomed.

Catherine filled me in later on what happened in Dr. Marcus' office. Our director sat speechless during Catherine's recitation.

"You received one of the kidnapper's letters and you didn't immediately report it? Why would you do such a thing? Your life was in danger," barked Dr. Marcus.

"I guess I thought I could get to the bottom of it myself. I was gonna' go with Joey," Catherine responded.

"Joey? Catherine, unless I'm mistaken, Joey doesn't have a badge. All right. We can't dwell on this. You have to tell the detectives every detail, so they can get to work on a plan. I'll get them into the office now. Don't move."

"Well, then I guess I should tell them about the second letter I received also," said Catherine timidly, under her breath.

By now, Dr. Marcus was exasperated. She called in the detectives and they took notes. Catherine spoke in detail about the new note being composed of letters from the cut out section of *Travel Magazine*, the three people who had purchased that magazine this morning, and seeing Lavinia's mom at school. Upon hearing this information, the detectives felt they were getting closer to the suspect. They put a watch on

Vunderfall and Uncle Mischa, then determined that setting up a sting operation, using Catherine, would be the most efficacious way to go.

The plan was to allow Catherine to meet the suspect at the tower at 8:00 P.M., install bugs on the tower door earlier in the day so they could hear everything while they hung out in one of the elevator shafts. If they heard that Catherine was in immediate danger, they'd surround the culprit. If it looked as though they'd be able to follow Catherine and the perpetrator to the other victims, they'd do that. All the while, Catherine would be wearing a wire so that all her moves could be monitored and could be responded to on a moment's notice—just like in the movies.

The day was drawing to a close. By 5:00 P.M. the weekly mass exodus from the lobby of students and faculty was complete. Catherine and I were told to meet in the director's office. Before our meeting, I called my uncle.

"Just checking in, Uncle Mischa. What are your plans tonight?"

"Mostly, to worry about you," he kidded.

"Other than that, Matti and I are taking in a, what do you kids call it, a flick and some dinner in the apartment. I can't really leave. The detectives are camped outside the building, watching my every move. It's most unsettling."

"Really? You and Matti and a flick?" I was amused and shocked. There was a picture for ya.

"Ah, she's a fine woman, you know. The only one I've ever met who can stand me! That makes her extremely attractive," he laughed. "She thinks I'm mysterious, imagine that!" I could hear his voice smiling.

I really couldn't believe my uncle was perhaps finally going to succumb to a relationship—albeit with someone who was taking care of him for much of his adult life. I guess they kind of matured together. Wow. Go Uncle Mischa!

"Well, don't do anything I wouldn't do," I said tritely. I didn't know what else to say. I was happy for him.

"And you be very careful, my boy. You're the closest I've ever come or ever will come to having a son. So don't blow it." I knew Uncle Mischa was serious and I loved him for it.

CHAPTER 20

THE STING

I hung up and met Cat at the office. They locked us in there with a plain-clothes detective. We had some sandwiches, brought to us from the cafeteria and we waited.

"Your uncle and Maestro Vunderfall will be watched all night tonight by police—just in case," remarked Catherine in a whisper.

"You know, when I came to the city this was not the kind of adventure I signed on for," I admitted.

"I know. Have you called your parents to tell them what's been happening?" asked Catherine

"Absolutely not. They'd have me home in two hours."

"Joey, make sure they don't let anything happen to me, OK? Don't let them wait too long to get me out of—wherever!"

Catherine was scared to death. I couldn't blame her. What started out as a fascinating curiosity to us could now end in a senseless debacle.

At 7:45 P.M. the other detectives entered the office. It was time. I was to come along in case they needed me as a decoy or for some other undisclosed purpose. Catherine stepped into a separate elevator from us. She had to be seen as taking this meeting alone. The police stopped our elevator just under the floor, without the numbers lighting up or making any sounds. We waited and listened. Cat was now walking through the halls, humming parts of the *Mendelssohn Violin Concerto*. It was her piece for the Junior Tchaikovsky Competition. It was the thing in our lives causing us the greatest stress at the moment beside this ridiculous charade. Noah, Gabriel, Lavinia, Cat, and I were chosen to compete in this nerve-devouring competition. We were the youngest performers ever allowed to appear.

What was the point of that? The school just wanted to have the honor of sending their first group of young talent, but everyone else in it was in upper high school and college. Why would they put a bunch of twelve and thirteen year olds through such harrowing tension? So many hours of study a day, upsetting violin lessons for months, extra accompanist rehearsals — which few of us could actually afford—stress!

How could we spend three to five hours a day practicing for this, go to school, do homework, finish projects on time, and study for our exams? Not to mention prepare for our Saturday classes. We didn't need to be doing such a thing at this point in our lives. Locked into a situation where our friends have no clue what we're up against, so they think we're freaks, our violin teachers know what we're up against and they keep pushing us so the judges will think they are extraordinary. Our parents and families are totally on the edge because they're torn between mediating our practice schedules with our school schedules and trying to pick up the pieces when we'd fall apart on a daily basis.

The humming continued. I was becoming nauseous. Static . . . suddenly only static. Where was Catherine?

CHAPTER 21

GOTCHA'

"What's wrong with the wire? Do you get a signal?" The taller officer asked the other.

"It's gotta' be a temporary problem. I checked all the equipment before I wired her," said the smaller, round one.

"Catherine, hey honey can you hear us?" whispered the taller.

Suddenly the sound of jangling and clanging was heard piercingly through the line.

"What is that? Where's that comin' from?" asked the taller.

It was the unmistakable sound of keys—and it was getting closer and closer to the elevator doors. The problem was we didn't know where Catherine was at that moment.

"Come on Catherine, give us a signal, honey. Tap on the wire, you don't have to speak," said the smaller officer.

Not a sound. Then a door slamming shut, no more keys, the whirring of the static persisted. The elevator next to us began moving down, one floor, two floors. Did it have Catherine in it? More importantly, did she have company?

The detectives were very quiet. They were figuring

out where the second elevator had gone.

"It's stopped in the basement. That's the janitor's area. That would explain the jangling keys and the door locking. He was probably putting supplies away for the night. He could still be here at this time, right?" the tall one asked his partner, as if he needed encouragement for his hypothesis.

The tall one was pretty quiet, he tapped on his mic a couple of times, shook it, blew in it and suddenly . . . well, there they were again . . . the notes to the third movement of *Mendelssohn.* It was Catherine, giving us a signal. She was all right. That was close. I was beginning to feel like we were in our own Spring horror flic, *The Disappearing Disciples, A Little Nightmare Music!, Terminator 4—At The Tower Door!* It was all so surreal.

"Now, don't say a word to us Catherine, just keep walking to the left of center, toward that huge door. If it's open now, give us a little sneeze."

"Ha-chooie" Catherine blasted over the mics. We all had a good laugh from that. She almost blew us right out of the shaft.

"Good one Cat," I piped in. "Next time say something like . . ."

"Oh my goodness! Lavinia, what are you doing here?" Cat shouted.

"Yeah, that's the idea. Drop us some name of this lunatic so we can get background on him, okay?" I whispered into the mic.

"You're supposed to be in China. How did you get into the tower? You've gotta' leave. Your life could be in danger. Don't you know what's been going on around here?"

Catherine either took me too seriously and was going to concoct a kidnapper to talk to, or she found the kidnapper and it was . . . LAVINIA!

"I wouldn't worry about me, Cat. I'm so glad you'll be joining us. The others have been waiting for you. I promise I'll tell you everything, but you have to come with me."

Son of a gun, it *was* Lavinia. The detectives and I looked at each other in complete disbelief. Never did they imagine that a student could have masterminded this chaos.

"Come with you where? And what others are you talking about?" Catherine asked in an annoyed tone of voice. She never had much patience for Lavinia.

"Oh, don't pretend you don't know—Gabriel, Noah, my friend Su-jin from, Juilliard. They have her doing this insane competition, too. She just joined us this afternoon. No one knows she's gone yet," giggled Lavinia.

"You think this is funny?" Catherine huffed. "Are you really the one responsible for all this?"

"Well, let's say it's a mutual appreciation club. You'll see when you get there. You'll love the idea."

"I'm not going anywhere with you until you tell me where we're going," Catherine insisted.

"To our little hideout, of course. There's nothing sinister going on here. We are just having a meaning-ful student revolt, Cat. The kids can't take the pres-sure anymore. Our teachers don't understand us, the administration doesn't care, as long as they produce a winner, our teachers are clueless to how miserable they're making our lives 'cause they have tunnel vision—their eyes' on the prize, and our parents are pushing and pushing as if we were horses in a race, neck and neck till we reach the gate—then they get to collect."

"Collect what? What are you talking about? The competition? You guys have gotten together to protest the Junior Tchaikovsky Competition by disappearing?"

"Exactly. I spearheaded the entire protest—well, me and my, uh, associate—and we had no trouble getting the others to join us. You were the toughest so far. It took two letters to catch your interest. We figured Joey would be the toughest, so we saved him for last. He's got the most ideals," Lavinia crowed!

"I just can't believe this. Do you know what anguish you're causing the parents and the conservatory?"

"Forget them! They have no idea what they're doing to us. What do they think, we're little performing robots—turn us on, we're perfect—turn us off we forget about the stress and roll merrily along on some other frequency?"

"We don't have to be doing this, Lavinia. There is still free will here."

"Oh, you don't get it. If we say no to our teachers, we will be perceived as failures; they'll never invite us to participate in any other challenges, they'll never give us the great music to play because they'll think we can't handle it yet. If we say no to our parents, we're considered disobedient and make them 'lose face' in the school and with our teachers. It's a lose/lose situation," asserted Lavinia.

There was a moment of silence. Cat must have been trying to collect her thoughts. She knew she had to calm down and follow Lavinia so there could be some closure to this whole awful situation.

"Okay, Lavinia, I get it. Let's go, I'm with you."

"Yes!" crowed Lavinia.

Another conquest. We heard the slamming of a door; it must have been the tower. They were on their way.

"Let's take the freight elevator down, just to be safe. No one usually takes that. The good part about this for you, Cat, is you only have to be away from your parents for the next two days. The competition is in three. My plan is to get Joey tomorrow."

"How do you think you'll do that? He's not at conservatory tomorrow. Didn't you get all the kids through notes in our mail slots?"

"Yeah, but he'll get one in his apartment mail box. I'll tell him if he ever wants to see you again, he better meet me. What do you think of that?"

"I think that stinks. Why should he care about that? He won't come."

"Duh, Catherine, he's so into you. He's crazy about you. Tell me you didn't know that. You must be the only one!" Lavinia laughed.

"To tell the truth, I'd never thought about Joey that way. I always saw him as a great friend."

" Hmmm . . ." cooed Lavinia, "you really missed the signals. Maybe that's worth pursuing, what do ya think?"

"Interesting," Catherine thought about this a moment . . . but just for a moment (never to be steered off track for long).

"Well, I still think it would take a lot more than that to have him get involved in this. He has put everything into practicing for this."

"Trust me. I know Joey. He'll do it—if you're connected to it," said Lavinia convincingly.

The sounds of the old, creaking freight elevator. Where were they headed?

"Ucch. It's dark and dank smelling down here. Where are we going?" asked Catherine suspiciously.

"There's a side exit here from the basement that will take us up a small flight of stairs. They'll bring us around the corner from the main entrance of the school. No one has seen me here in three weeks. I'd like to keep it that way."

They were in the basement of the conservatory. So Lavinia really had all the details taken care of. She had, no doubt, entered the school late in the afternoon through the basement, remained hidden till after hours, then moved carefully upstairs to her meeting area. It was very risky. She was just lucky she pulled it off this far."

When Cat and Lavinia emerged from the school they evidently entered a waiting car.

"A taxi? You called a taxi?" Catherine's voice rose an octave.

Who would imagine that, a yellow cab get-away car!

"Well, it'll get us where we've gotta' go," Lavinia countered.

We heard an engine start, and then the sounds of the road.

Catherine said nothing. The smaller officer mentioned that there had been an unmarked vehicle parked across the street from the taxi, watching it for the past few hours. They had been patrolling the area and noticed that both the cab and the driver hadn't moved for a couple of hours. They radioed the information to "my" officers. On the taller officer's order, the car would now follow our suspect until their final destination. We left the building as soon as we heard them leave.

We received directions from the undercover officers all the way to—Short Hills, New Jersey? That's what the exit sign said. That was where Lavinia lived. Within minutes after exiting, however, we found ourselves in a heavily forested area. We drove about ten more minutes and there, across the tracks, tucked into a well-treed alcove on the right hand side of the road, was a shabby, grey shingled motel, with a flashing neon sign that was missing a letter. It read: "V-cancy." It had a drive up parking lot in the front. All the rooms were facing the street, with old, peeling white numbers on them. I was ready to see a sign saying "Bates Motel!" What a great setting this was for a mystery. Someone had a finely tuned sense of drama to pick this place.

We pulled in behind the "undercover" car, about ten steps down the road from the motel driveway but still in plain sight. The yellow cab was parked in the driveway. The taller officer radioed the unmarked car, rattled off some directions and code numbers, and the unmarked car immediately pulled into the driveway behind the cab.

Lavinia and Cat got out of the car, but didn't spot us. We waited for them to enter their motel room. What was Lavinia doing at a motel, anyway? They walked up to the second floor and knocked on the third door from the landing. It opened slowly. . . . It was Gabriel. Behind him stood Noah and another girl I didn't recognize. I assumed it was Su-Jin. The detectives looked at each other as if to say, "What next?" They walked in quickly. We began to pick up the sounds of their conversation.

They wanted to get each of the kids on tape if they could—as evidence in this bizarre case. Now we were all waiting for just the right moment to "move in." (Nothing like this ever happened in Southbury).

Sure enough, through the wire we could hear that Catherine was surrounded by the whole group.

"Noah, Gabe, and you must be Su-jin. Oh, it's so good to see you all—well!" ("Alive" is the word she was thinking of!)

They all began hurling questions at Catherine, eager to get the inside scoop as to what had been going on at the school. Was the director fuming? Had she seen their parents? That was the only catch in this interestingly derived plot. Apparently, none of the kids really wanted to take part in scaring their parents half to death—but the cause—the cause was worth it, they thought. At least that's what Lavinia had told them. They were planning on reappearing at the conservatory the day of the Junior Tchaikovsky Competition. They'd enter the school with banners and a ready TV film crew, they explained.

"You can't get a TV crew to cover this, you'll ruin A.I.M. It'll create a scandal. Get your message across from within your own ranks. Just sit down in Dr. Marcus' office and tell her why you, uh, I mean we did it. Then she'll call our parents and teachers and they'll all be so thrilled that we've returned, they'll see it as a serious protest and they'll never let it happen again," Catherine pleaded.

"Well, maybe you're right about the TV thing. I wouldn't want to damage the conservatory in any way. Just teach them a lesson," added Lavinia.

Catherine obviously knew she had to get them talking so the police would have all their voices on record. She got right down to work.

"Let's all sit down, okay?"

A momentary shuffling.

"So, Gabriel, was it really too hard to keep up with school and your practicing for the competition? I mean, I know I've been stressed to the max, but I've been trying my best."

"Yes, well, we all have. I have it a little easier than most of you because I'm home schooled. I never set foot inside a school. My parents didn't let me. In Puerto Rico, I started violin at three, and, evidently, it was like breathing for me. I just took to it, you know?

"By the time I was six, my parents were dragging me from competition to competition. Of course, they wouldn't have been doing it if I hadn't been winning! They pulled me and pushed me all across Latin America. I won them all, first prize, second prize, statues, ribbons, plaques, money—that was the most important. But I always wanted to go to school like the other kids, play ball, see movies. Never. My parents had a plan, and it only included me peripherally. I was there to win. Win so you can get to America and study with the greats, win so you could get to American Institute of Music, win so you will be famous, win so our lives can be better.

"I started having nightmares from the time I was

seven. They were so real. I would dream that I'd go out on stage, the orchestra would begin and I'd forget my first notes, or I'd get so petrified I'd stand in place without even raising my violin, or I'd be playing splendidly then my fingers would miss a run and everyone would hear it. The audience would let out an audible gasp, followed by hushed whispers. My family and friends would hear it. They'd hear I wasn't really the best. The best wouldn't make mistakes with a whole orchestra behind him. I'd wake up in a cold sweat. This would happen once every couple of months— usually before competitions. It had become a way of life—a sick way of life.

"My days have been so full of journeys. The sad thing is that, if I do really make a concert career for myself within the next couple of years, that part will only get worse. I'll be traveling for the rest of my life. But . . . my parents will finally be able to afford a house, a car that doesn't beg for mercy every time the ignition key is turned, and they'll have proper respect in the family.

"I was even feeling a little happiness here at American Institute because I was just allowed to practice without pressure. Learn from my teacher without preparing a concert program every two months. I love the music, you know. I don't know anything else. It makes me happy, when it's just me and my music, on the stage together or in a practice room learning the next exciting movement of something—for no reason except to learn.

"So, when my teacher entered me into this Junior Tchaikovsky competition, all of my nightmares came flooding back to me. It has been a horrible time, these last few weeks. I couldn't bear to face my parents. How could I give up on them now?"

Everyone listened to Gabriel and gave him much empathy. They each had their own albatross to bear. Each was so compelling.

Su-jin spoke next. Apparently she had come from Korea with her family this past year. She was the new star violinist in her country, and her teacher convinced her parents to pack up and move their lives to America. Su-jin lived in poverty in her little town. Her father had been a violinist but presently was out of work. There was little money being given to orchestras now, and they had to cut back. Her parents brought her to the biggest violin teacher in the country when she was five years old because her father thought she showed such promise. He had been teaching Su-jin since she was two and a half years old. The violin teacher took her as a student immediately—on total scholarship.

"I remember coming home from school at 2:00 in the afternoon in Korea, then going right to my room to practice. I practiced till 6:00 P.M. without a break. Then I'd have dinner and practice another two hours before I was even allowed to do my school home work. When I was too tired to go on playing, my father would come in and threaten to paddle me. I cried and cried, listening to him talking about honor and respect, and discipline. When he finished, I dried my eyes, picked up the violin and played for the rest of my required time. My teacher could see the water stains on the varnish of my violin. She asked my father to stop making me cry so much.

"Finally, when I became twelve, my violin teacher

told my parents we must move to America so that I could attend Juilliard or A.I.M. If I was going to become a great concert artist, that had to be my path. I had friends who had made the trip and were so happy. They loved their new teachers in America, loved conservatory, and even their parents became more relaxed once they were settled on their path. My parents, dutiful as always, agreed to make this life change, and within two weeks, our house was sold, I said my last goodbyes to friends in school, and off we went to America. My mother even had to sell her wedding ring to afford plane tickets for the three of us. It is a big responsibility I have now, you understand. I love my life here, and I must become a great violinist, not just excellent. Excellent is not good enough for all they've given up for me."

Catherine couldn't take it anymore.

"All they've given up for you? What about all you've given up in your life? You and Gabriel both! You've given up everything. It doesn't come back to you, you know. Once these years are gone, they're gone. You can't have a life made up of practice and nothing else. You guys will burn out before you're twenty," she exclaimed.

"Catherine, it's nice of you to care, but in our families, the goals are established and we must bring them honor. This, however, is just too much, this competition. We are too young to beat out those high school and college students, and our teachers know that. Yet they expect that we do nothing in our lives for this whole past two months but practice our concerto. I've lost so many days of school because I needed more time to practice to get it to a professional level. In my country you do competitions within your age range. A twelve or thirteen year old doesn't compete with an eighteen year old. I feel like I'm drowning here. I had to join Lavinia—for my sanity, for my self-respect."

"What will your parents do to you?" asked Catherine with concern.

"What can they do to me that hasn't already been done?" responded Su-jin sadly.

Next it was Noah's turn to speak. As was characteristic for Noah, he began his story by getting a bit teary eyed.

"I was home schooled too, you know, for a long time. I never had to interact with another kid my age if I didn't want to, until 7th grade, when my parents relented and sent me to middle school. Everything I needed was either at my violin teacher's studio or in my house. My parents were so into how much music I could learn and how quickly that I barely got through my math and science curriculum each year. Those were considered 'disposable income!' As long as my fingers were working, the rest of me didn't seem to matter.

"I certainly enjoyed not having to take tests, but I missed out on a lot of popular culture. I always thought that 'pop culture' meant culture from my grandpa's time. With this kind of upbringing, what could I have ever said to a kid my age? 'Hey, what did ya think of that Emerson Trio?' or 'Boy, Joshua Bell hit a home run with that concerto last night at Lincoln Center!' or 'So, who do you think does a better Bruch?—Midori or Zuckerman?' They'd all look at me like I was an alien life form or something.

"So, I found it increasingly more comfortable not to associate with kids at all. I was actually nervous about starting conservatory because it meant I'd have to be around kids all day. Imagine what I felt like—inside all day every Saturday, taking theory class, sight singing class, music history, conducting class, scale class, performance workshop, two hours of orchestra and one hour of chamber music, composition class—and I'll let ya all in on a little secret—I hated it! I hated it all! I hated music. I never asked for this. I was a little kid when this was all thrust on me. I was supposed to please everybody. So I did. I became a technical wonder. But that wasn't enough. My teachers always told me I sounded empty inside; that I was playing all the right notes with all the right strokes but no music was coming out.

" 'Oh, you'll learn how to emote as you mature,' some of the faculty would say. I heard that one a lot. But I wouldn't learn. I had nothing inside to emote. Empty as a clamshell without its tenant. There's no returning from that—and *this* clam knows it. At least I finally got to go to middle school with the rest of the kids in my neighborhood. I saw what I had been missing all these years."

I couldn't believe what I was hearing through the tap. Who knew he had been so miserable in his life. We just thought he had no self esteem. What was he thinking? He was thirteen years old. When was he going to stand up to his parents? Listening to these poor kids' lives made me feel embarrassingly normal. It felt good to belong to an endeavor that suited me. I loved my music. No one pushed me. They supported me—big difference! I knew so many kids in conservatory who just loved being there too. We'd look forward from Saturday to Saturday to see our friends, to hear great music coming from each other, to learn the next part of whatever exciting concerto we were working on—to be musicians together in the right environment. Juilliard, A.I.M.— these were the places music lovers were made; whether they became the future's great soloists or the future's cultured concert goers didn't matter to our institutions. As long as they educated the next generation's major talent. It was a pleasure for most of us to be part of that. As for the nonsense that accompanied being a serious music student—well, every field has its tough to handle parts. Even the social scene was a challenge, and I was hoping that it would iron itself out by high school. Without challenge there is no reward— right? What's the point?

Catherine listened to these sagas quietly. I know she must have felt awful. She was a "lifer." She was someone who loved her art and couldn't conceive of anyone having such pain as a musician. That was her nature. As for Lavinia, she didn't say a word. We all knew her story anyway, and it wasn't pretty either.

It was up to Catherine to get them to talk about the pseudo-kidnapping now. The police needed to hear the whole plan before they could move in.

"So you guys had just had it, huh? Did you decide to run away together or something? I mean, how did you pull this off? Where'd you get the money?"

Now Lavinia piped up. "It was all my idea—well, and Gabriel's. We planned the whole thing down to the last detail. See, I would pretend to run away to China. I had all that money for my round trip ticket to China that I never used. You'd be surprised how long you could live off that in a cheap motel. Pretty cagey, huh? Then we'd get the other four contenders (we had expected Joey would join us in the end), for the Junior Tchaikovsky Competition to hide out with us, telling them that if we all banded together and stayed away from the competition, we wouldn't have to worry about the stress of practice. The day of the competition, we'd show ourselves again. It would only be for a couple of weeks."

"But the postcards your mom said she got from China, signed by you?"

"Ah, that was the best plan. I asked my grandma in China to send me a few blank postcards of some of the wonderful places I'd see when I'd come, so I could get a feel for the place, you know? I never gave her an exact date that I'd be arriving. Since I always got home before my mom each day, I'd make sure to grab the mail and remove the cards before she'd notice. Then, I'd write my little notes on them to my mother. So, when I actually left home, I returned one week later at 6:00 A.M. to put the first card in our mailbox. She never knew the difference. I put stamps from China on the cards, so Mom never noticed they hadn't been postmarked. It's too expensive to call China, so as long as my mom got a couple of cards, she was happy."

"Wow. Didn't you guys think about what you were putting your parents through, though? How could some of you just disappear for a couple of weeks and think that your parents would be okay with it? They think you're all dead! Kidnapped! A statistic! Are you out of your minds?"

Catherine's voice rose steadily in a crescendo as if

she was phrasing a great musical ascending passage. "If you didn't want to do the competition, why didn't you have your parents talk to your teachers? You're in charge of your own lives!" Catherine chastised them.

There was silence on the tap. Nobody spoke for a few seconds. Maybe they had never fully thought it through before.

"Were you going to appear at home and expect no questions to be asked? You'll be chopped liver by the time they get finished with you. Worse—you'll have wished you were practicing eight hours a day for a month. Anything will be better than what you're gonna' face."

Su-jin then explained that she expects to return to Korea and live with her cousins. They already gave her permission. She was not going to continue her life this way with her parents. Gabriel thought he was making a strong statement as well by doing this protest—one that his parents would have to pay attention to.

"They are not bad people. They just never understood how much pressure I was under all the time. I think they'll change their expectations. I don't want to leave the field. I want to be great. Just not right this minute," Gabriel admitted.

Noah became quite impassioned. He had just done something that was impulsive for the first time in his life and it felt good. He didn't think about what would happen down the line. "I have been more relaxed during the past couple of weeks than I can ever remember. These guys understand me. They understand me. Don't you, Catherine? You understand too, right? I couldn't go on any other way," he gushed.

It was truly pitiful—and actually a bit ominous.

What would Noah have done if this plan had not come along? How much longer before he totally cracked under the pressure?

"Look, if we return next week, we do so as a unit in protest. Some things have to change. Kids cannot be treated as adults in this field and be expected to withstand the same pressures. If you're talented you need to be nurtured, not pitted one against the other. You need to make music, to be allowed to express yourselves, to take time," Lavinia crowed.

Who'd have ever pictured Lavinia as an activist.

"Well, I have a real problem with the way you've gone about it," said Catherine in her most mature Catherine-like parlance, "but I do agree with your motives. It has been next to impossible keeping up with everything. But don't be surprised if they throw you out of American Institute for this little trick. You know one thing about being prodigious, there's always someone new waiting in the wings to dethrone you. It may take a year or two to find, but there'll be a new bumper crop just dying to take your places."

"What are they gonna' do, kick us all out?" asked Lavinia self-righteously. "That's not happening. Anyway, you're part of the plan now, Catherine. You're sworn to secrecy till after the competition. If you join us, you could save me a letter and call Joey. Get him to sign on. Then we'll have the solid front we need," continued Lavinia.

"Oh, sorry, I'm not joining this, and Joey would never go for it. He's way too level headed. Besides, we've put too much preparation into it already. We have to try out," Catherine explained.

"And what was with those scary letters you sent,

like a serial killer—all cut out from magazines, singed by fire. Why didn't you just go around asking everyone?" Catherine continued.

"It wouldn't have made the impact," Lavinia answered.

This was all the police had to hear. They surrounded the perimeter of the motel and broke the silence of the night with their megaphones: "This is the police. All right kids, come out of the room and no one will be hurt. You're surrounded."

"How could this be? How were we followed? No one has found us for three weeks. It must have been a trap. Catherine, did you set us up?"

Catherine was definitely feeling outnumbered right about now. "Of course not. Why would I do such a thing? I didn't know it was going to be you, Lavinia, hiding out in the tower."

"Exactly, maybe you thought you'd crack the case and have the police follow you somehow. No, I know, you figured if you had us put away, you and Joey would have the competition all to yourselves," Lavinia ranted.

"Lavinia, you're out of your mind. I had no way of knowing you guys were all in cahoots. And anyway, isn't the whole point of your protest to demonstrate that this was a waste of twelve and thirteen year old energy, since we'd never win this level of competition against college students?" Catherine tried admirably to unravel herself from the net of guilt she was snagged in.

"Well, we had better get out there before they get trigger happy," said Gabriel, seemingly resigned to his fate.

"They're not shooting anybody. We're just kids. We'll get off," huffed Lavinia

Lavinia went to the door first, with the rest, sullenly, following behind. I stayed hidden in one of the police cars so no one would suspect Catherine or myself of a sting operation. My parents would never believe this. The police rounded up Gabe, Noah, and Su-jin into one car; they placed Lavinia in another, and Catherine came in mine. We gave each other a huge hug. We couldn't help ourselves.

I *thought, at that moment, of Greg whom I had met on the train coming to Manhattan. I wondered if he found someone else's life to write about, or if he had made his own. You never know what's going to happen in life, do you?*

The upshot of this whole experience was that Cat and I did the Junior Tchaikovsky Competition. We got fantastic scores and jury comments, but, as we expected, took home no prizes—that is, except one . . . we knew we had done it. We worked, we pushed ourselves, we didn't crack, we excelled, and we'd be back. We had achieved something tremendously satisfying in life—ownership. We knew exactly who we were, and could be proud of it.

I called my mom, dad and grandma when it was all over. I read them my jury grades and comments. They were very pleased. I know you're wondering if I ever told them about the mystery at A.I.M. . . . That would come to be my greatest secret. I learned from Uncle Mischa, being a man of mystery can be quite compelling.

So what happened to Lavinia and the "crew?" Well, the administration suspended the kids for the rest of

241

the semester, and put them on one year's probation; meaning no monkey business for a year. They would be watched carefully and all had to maintain an A average in their courses. What happened to each of them when their parents got them home, I just couldn't say, but I was sure I'd find out in the Fall.

One good thing that did come out of this adventure was that the administration and the faculty had numerous meetings in the month of June regarding the psychological well being of its students. It's not that they had never thought about it before. My teacher, Ms. Liebling, for example, was extremely conscious about not pushing her students beyond their limits. She had keen antennae and could tell when you were at the breaking point. Still, she had to go along with what the administration expected. She had some of the most talented students in the school under her tutelage. A great deal of success was expected from them. Everything, ultimately, reflected on her. That can't be easy for a teacher. Still, we were the ones under the gun.

The director, Dr. Marcus, decided that no one under sixteen would ever be sent to major international competitions unless the student, not the parent, asked for this honor in writing. If a student was willing to put himself through the rigor of such training, then it was all right with the conservatory.

The faculty also agreed to dispense a list of all students involved in major orchestral debuts and competitions throughout the year. This way each teacher would know what the students were going through and they could waive homework assignments and tests to lessen the students' burdens. Now this was a great concession. If only our public school system would act in such a humane and understanding way. Not that we wanted to be treated differently, it's just that this world of ours, music, is extremely demanding both physically (like an athlete's), and mentally. When we work in conservatory for five or six hours, it's equivalent to taking a test in school from 7:30 A.M. till the final bell, with four or five 5 minute breaks thrown in. That's how consistent our mental energy must be.

In light of all this, it was a good thing to have our music faculty on our side. Lavinia and her heinous stunt did wind up opening some eyes. I guess A.I.M. felt that if its students would go to such lengths for attention, they better attend to them. Lavinia actually turned out to be a trail blazer. What a year!

It was June 7th. Conservatory was over. I spent my lunch period with the crew: Lavinia, Gabe, Noah and, of course, Catherine. We reviewed the year in depth: the departure of Valery, the competition, the various concerts, my moments of fame on national television and in the papers, the firing of Vunderfall, the eccentricities of Mischa Golub, and the pseudo-kid-nappings. My year also, unfortunately, included the death of Zayde. He would have been so proud of my endeavors. I still couldn't believe he wouldn't be with me at Lincoln Center for my debut in October. But Grandma would be, and he'd be there in my mind, on that stage, inside my music.

We talked about summer plans. Catherine was going to study with a highly-esteemed faculty of world-renowned violinists in a famous Canadian Music Festival, then return home to vacation with her family. Lavinia, who had wanted to go to Meadowmount was, instead, invited to tour in Beijing, Shanghai, and Hong Kong as a soloist. I thought that was much better than going to a summer music program. Gabriel was actually being allowed to do a non-music program this summer. He was playing tennis at a camp in Puerto Rico and living with his cousins. He promised his parents he'd be practicing every day, but without a goal. What a concept? Noah was in the process of discussing a great compromise with his parents. They felt he had too much talent to give up violin, but he wanted to chuck it for the summer and see the world; so they were sending him to an exciting, nurturing, and relaxed environment with other young musicians, in the hope that he'd come to enjoy and mature in his talent. They were sending him to Europe for one month to study chamber music in Italy. He would be with kids his own age, be able to take side trips all over Italy, and learn his craft at the same time. What a deal for Noah. Maybe I should try this on my folks!

Lavinia said that her friend, Su-jin, was accepted to a young concert artists' program in Austria to study and perform Mozart all summer—a Mozart Festival of sorts. She was happy about it because it would be away from her parents. I would spend the summer playing some golf and tennis in Connecticut, and preparing for the greatest musical moment of my life—Lincoln Center. I couldn't complain. I think that we all did extremely well.

I had two more weeks of school and then it would be home to Connecticut. I could hardly believe it. Although I was totally ready for a break, I was sad to leave my uncle and friends. I knew I'd be back in less than three months, but not living in Manhattan—just studying at A.I.M. My one consolation in leaving Uncle Mischa was that he would be well taken care of. He and Matti were now an item.

"So Uncle Mischa, does this mean you'll finally let Matti into your studio?" I asked.

"If she promises not to mess with my leprechauns," quipped my uncle. "No body cleans in my studio and lives!" he laughed.

"Ah, exasperating man," sighed Matti with a smile. She loved him. She couldn't help herself.

I called my mom and dad and told them I'd be coming home on the 21st, after finals. They were planning a big homecoming with a special dinner, my favorite desserts, a movie, and good old fashioned shmoozing. Then I called Grandma.

"So?"

"So what?"

"So what was it like living with your Uncle Mischa? Was he good to you? Did he help you? Did he think you had promise?"

"Grandma, Uncle Mischa is amazing. He's a brilliant violinist, he's a character who defies color, he's exotic . . ."

"Mischa is exotic? My Mischa?"

"Yes Grandma, he's very unusual, and he's very loving."

"Ah, now you've made me happy. Your zayde would have been so glad to hear that. He never found anyone to love, you know, my poor Mischa."

"Well, I think that's gonna' change."

"You know something?"

"I know nothing."

"You know something."

I'm just extrapolating."

"From what?"

"It's just a feeling, Grandma. And by the way, I heard all about your 'underwear' technique for getting him to practice. Don't even think of trying that on me."

"Don't worry, ziskeit, I have a whole new line of techniques for you. I'm just getting started."

I knew she wasn't kidding and I was looking forward to the entire experience. Such a grandma. Never was there such a grandma.

The 21st came. I sent an E-mail off to Catherine before she left for the summer. I told her to hold onto her seat for next year. It's bound to be exciting. I had come to expect the unexpected at A.I.M. She E-mailed me back to call her at the end of August, before school.

"Sounds promising," I thought.

I packed, had my last brunch of scrambled eggs and cheese made by Matti, and left for the train station with my uncle in his Chevy.

"Uncle Mischa, can I ask you something?"

"Uh-oh, sounds serious. Fire away."

"Are you ever sorry for having given up so much of your life for the music? I mean, you went through such hard times because of it."

"Ah, there's where you're wrong, my dear boy. My hard times were never because of music. They were because of people. Music can only make your soul sing. It is the antidote for homework, tests, traffic, stupidity. Only people can bring you hard times. They are the culprits. In fact, Joey, it was my music that got me through it all."

"But you gave every hour of your life to become a great, renowned violinist, and it was taken from you in the end. It wasn't even your fault. You had it all, and it was taken."

"Joey, blaming music for that is like blaming God for the Nazis or the terrorists. God is goodness. Music, is beauty. They're both miracles, really. Only people can hurt us and keep our world from wholeness. Whether you choose to believe me now is totally up to you, but I feel more whole now than I ever did. I teach the beauty to other young artists, I have the luck of feeling love again when I thought it was hopeless, and I have gotten to know, mentor and adore Josef Cohen, my brilliantly talented nephew, who will bring new life to the world with his fiddle."

"So there's no more glass shattering in your life, Uncle?"

"I've found my peace, Joey. It can take a lifetime, and look how lucky I am that I've found it now? Many people live their lives in quiet desperation, and you don't even know who they are. *They* don't even know who they are. But one day they wake up and can't hear the music in their lives. They become very sad. You will not let that happen. You will not let idiots keep you from your path. You will not let difficulties keep you from your path. You will not let failure keep you from this path either."

I listened to my uncle as if every word was going to fall off the face of the earth and never be heard again. I caught them, hastily, greedily, and held them in my heart, in a place where nay sayers can't enter; *deep inside . . . where the music is.*

ABOUT THE AUTHOR

Jourdan Urbach—13 year old concert violinist Jourdan Urbach has been compared to a "Young Paganini" with "buttery smooth playing" by New York critics. Jourdan has performed frequently in solo recitals at major concert halls in the New York Metropolitan area, including Carnegie Recital Hall, Lefrak Hall, Steinway Hall, and The Tilles Center. He has also appeared as soloist with The New Haven Symphony, The Park Avenue Chamber Symphony, The Metropolitan Youth Orchestra, and The Massapequa Philharmonic.

Jourdan made his Lincoln Center Debut on October 22, 2003 as soloist with the Park Avenue Chamber Symphony, performing *The Bruch Violin Concerto* (Charles Osgood of CBS News was emcee, and Reynolds Levy, President of Lincoln Center, honored Jourdan in his introduction). His performance was also featured on WQXR's *Young Artist Showcase,* where host Robert Sherman noted that Jourdan was "The one to watch for the future; a brilliant performer."

Jourdan has an exciting and aggressive concert schedule this season, including his Carnegie Hall Debut (Main Stage), as soloist with the Park Avenue Chamber Symphony, performing the *Sibelius Violin Concerto* on January 19, 2005. He will also be a featured performer at the Kravis Center in Palm Beach, Florida on January 16, 2005, in a Gala Concert Special for *From the Top,* the national classical radio show which highlights America's musical prodigies.

Jourdan has been a featured guest artist on national television, performing and being interviewed on *Good Morning America* by Diane Sawyer; *The Caroline Rhea Show; CNN—Lou Dobbs Tonight; Inside Edition* with Deborah Norville; and *Last Call With Carson Daly. The New York*

Times, The Daily News and Newsday have published substantial profiles of Jourdan, focusing both on his accomplishments as a concert violinist and author. Jourdan's first novel, *Leaving Jeremiah (Goose River Press)*, is now in its second printing.

Jourdan was also featured in *People Magazine* on April 12, 2004 in a profile article entitled, *"Young People Who Will Make America's Future."*

Jourdan studies the violin privately with Patinka Kopec, and is a student in The Juilliard School's Pre-College Division studying under Lewis Kaplan.

Jourdan is the founder of CHC (Children Helping Children), a musical charity foundation which fundraises for New York area hospitals and medical organizations and has raised tens of thousands of dollars for pediatric divisions all over New York. Proceeds from Jourdan's Carnegie Hall Debut in January, 2005 will go to benefit The National Multiple Sclerosis Society.

Jourdan has received citations from The Nassau County and New York State Legislatures for his accomplishments in the fields of music and literature, as well as for his great humanitarian work with CHC. Jourdan's future goal is to pursue a career in neurosurgery and he will be attending Johns Hopkins University this summer for study in neuroscience, as he was chosen to be a participant in the Johns Hopkins University Center for Talented Youth. Jourdan's present goal is to make a difference in the lives of as many children under hospital care as possible, with his music and fundraising.

Jourdan Urbach is a courageous, brilliantly skillful 13 year old fictioneer. His second novel, *Inside the Music,* takes a firm stand regarding the overwhelming expectations set on young, extraordinary achievers, particularly violin prodigies. Jourdan's wisdom and courage are evident in the profound ethical and psychological questions he raises concerning: prodigious guilt, anxieties about peer acceptance, the tenuous support system of teachers and great mentors in the upper echelons of music, and tactics used by parents to give their child a competitive edge. All of this is done with great humor, suspense, literary craft, and thought provoking dialogue from characters every teen reader needs to know. *Inside the Music* is a memorable story and powerful contribution to the fields of literature, music, education, psychology and parenting. Bravo, Jourdan!

—*Victoria Nesnick, Founder, The Kids Hall of Fame*

Reading this book, one cannot help thinking of J.K. Rowling and her Harry Potter series of novels, except that this takes place in a music conservatory. What do the worlds of magic and music have in common? Jourdan Urbach—the engaging author and 13 year old violin prodigy who actually lives *Inside the Music* every day, and practices his magic at Juilliard (not at Hogwarts), and on concert stages throughout the nation. His wand is his bow, and he, like Harry, never ceases to create warm and lasting friendships among his classmates and mentors. Although this is fiction, one of the great gifts of this dynamic, heartfelt story is that the reader cannot help but get to know the author through his protagonist, Joey—a sensitive, intelligent and extraordinarily talented young man who makes everyone feel special and who never lets you down. I recommend this book highly to every parent and child who wants to appreciate what it takes to make magic in music.

—*David Bernard, Music Director & Conductor,*
The Park Avenue Chamber Symphony

There are prodigies in every field, but how many of them are of equal talent in several fields? And how many have been featured on national television numerous times as well as in all the major newspapers by the age of twelve? Jourdan Urbach, the brilliant violinist whose great prodigiousness spans the fields of music, science, literature, language and philanthropy, gives us a rare opportunity to witness the thrilling and competitive world of musical prodigy. You will be captivated by his characters and the heart and humor with which they must go through life—all trying to be the best! It is a story that needs to be read by kids in every field, and with every talent and dream.

—*Patinka Kopec, Violin & Viola Faculty,*
Manhattan School of Music
Associate to Pinchas Zukerman
Performance Program (M.S.M.)
Co-Director National Arts Center, Canada
Faculty, Perlman Music Program